I0640162

# Space Commando

## The Seven Stars Universe, Volume 2

Dayne Edmondson

Published by Dark Star Publishing, 2020.

SPACE COMMANDO

**First edition. November 20, 2020.**

Copyright © 2020 Dayne Edmondson.

ISBN: 978-1393338154

Written by Dayne Edmondson.

# Also by Dayne Edmondson

**The Dark Tide Trilogy**
Emergence
Eclipse
Ruin

**The Mageborn Saga**
Mageborn
The Cursed Tower
Halls of Light

**The Magical Madelyn Mayfield**
Madelyn and the Unicorn Beach

**The Seven Stars Universe**
Ghost Ranger
Space Commando

**The Shadow Trilogy**
Blood and Shadows
Time of Shadows
Shadows Fall


**Standalone**
The Complete Dark Tide Trilogy
The Complete Shadow Trilogy


Watch for more at https://www.darkstarpublishing.com.

# Chapter 1

"They've hit the top turret!" the first mate shouted through the intercom. "There's too many of them!"

I gritted my teeth and wished the ship-wide intercom system had a volume control, or that they didn't feel the need to announce every battle update to the entire ship. It was hard to hear myself think with how loud the man was. I watched on the tactical display as the bottom turret fired at our pursuers. Of course, the first mate didn't trust me, their hired gun, to use the ship-mounted guns. No, he wanted it all to himself while I twiddled my thumbs.

"Putting more power to the engines," the captain said. "We have to try to outrun them." His voice cracked, which suggested to me he was panicking.

I'd only been aboard the *Voltir* for a week, but I'd gotten a read on most of the crew of the merchant ship in that time. The captain was a sleazy wheeling and dealing con artist who relied on his brother, the first mate, to intimidate his crew into obedience. The first mate was a womanizing ass who couldn't land a deal to save his life. The rest of the crew consisted of general laborers who were too busy drinking to notice the new security guard.

The ship jerked and that security guard, me, almost flew against the bulkhead. Only a burst of gravitic energy kept me in position. I let out a sigh of frustration and clicked the intercom. "Captain, open the top airlock at my signal. I'll take care of the enemy ships."

"Do you have a death-wish, lass?" the first mate asked. "Think your corpse is gonna destroy one of those fighters?"

*What do you care if I do?* I thought. The man had shown barely any interest toward me after I'd shoved his hand away during our first meeting. I guess that was preferable to him being lecherous, but still, there was no love lost between us. Instead, I said, "I have a plan. Just be ready."

He grunted loudly enough to be heard through the intercom. "Fine. It's your funeral."

"And some coin back in our pocket," the captain chimed in.

I rolled my eyes and set my weapons on the floor. I wouldn't need them where I was going. Then I climbed the stairs toward the central lift. The laborers sat strapped into their transit seats, and I felt a few pairs of eyes, and mutters of "fool," "too pretty to die" and "who's that" following me.

Entering the lift, I sealed it and welcomed relief from the intercom. At least until I activated it in the lift - the only place you could turn the bloody thing on and off other than the privy. "I'm ready. Activate the lift."

"You're not in a spacesuit," the first mate replied.

I looked up to where the camera watched me. "I don't need one. I'm dead, remember?" Technically undead, but at that moment I preferred to emphasize the part that made it clear I didn't need air to survive. One of my physical characteristics that kept most merchant vessels from hiring me could end up saving the ship and her crew.

"Aye, I remember," he said. "Just don't damage my ship."

"Our ship," the captain said.

The first mate didn't reply to his brother. "Raising the lift."

The tube jerked and I rose toward the top of the ship. The cargo lift, used to ferry goods into the ship, would now be used to ferry me to my enemies. *They won't know what hit them.* I drew upon my power to bind myself to the floor of the lift as the door above my head slid open and all air in the tube evacuated. The sounds of explosions and absorption of energy, of crew speech and the infernal intercom, faded to silence. Blissful silence.

The floor of the tube now sat even with the top of the ship. I did not waver as the ship performed a sharp evasive maneuver, my gravity power holding me as steady as if I were held by military-grade mag-boots.

Resisting the urge to draw breath, a persistent, if unnecessary habit that still hadn't disappeared completely, I released gravity's hold on my body and shot backward, binding upward to keep the ship's exhaust from scorching me. Then, setting my sights on six enemy fighters flashing past me at several thousands of kilometers per second, I bound myself in their direction, *hard*.

I soared through space, velocity causing my hair to flap behind me and my cheeks to feel as though they were peeling back. I accelerated to a speed faster than the pursuing fighters and closed on them. I hadn't had time to experiment on the range of my gravity-manipulation powers, so the closer I could get the better my expected results.

I came so close to the first fighter I could see the skull symbol painted atop their helmet through the canopy. *Now*, I thought, splitting my attention between the binding pulling me forward and a new binding on the target fighter. An aura of darkness, visible only to my eyes, surrounded the fighter. Then, imagining tendrils growing out from the aura, I attached them like a rope to its wing-mate.

Within moments, the wing-mate of the original fighter jerked, and its engines flared with greater brightness as it tried to fight the force of gravity emanating from my first target. It lost the fight and tumbled end-over-end, like a cart-wheeling gymnast, crashing into the other fighter and causing a brief-lived fireball to flare into existence.

*Two down, four to go.*

A stream of thick light flashed from behind me and pierced the space ahead of me.

*Make that four fighters and their home ship,* I amended silently.

The distraction of my presence gave the *Voltir* an opening. They barrel-rolled and their bottom guns spurt coilgun shells toward their pursuers. One stream of the superheated material sliced through one of the fighters, leaving three. Fifty percent losses among the enemy within two minutes of me joining the battle weren't too shabby.

The death of a third comrade shook the remaining fighters out of their shock, however, and they spread to avoid both my magic and the guns of the ship I'd been hired to protect. I wouldn't be able to use the same trick twice.

*But I can go for the jugular,* I thought. I set my gaze on the larger ship that had spewed the enemy fighters and laser beam from earlier forth. Looking like a retrofitted freighter, it hung back, watching, perhaps ready to cut its losses and run if the *Voltir* continued to beat the odds. With luck, they'd miss me flying toward them.

I formed a singularity in front of me and bound myself to it. Then I hurled it toward the large freighter-turned-pirate-home-ship and braced myself as it dragged me along.

The singularity neared the enemy ship at a frightening speed. I lost track of the movement of the enemy fighters as I zeroed in on my target. I was within a few hundred kilometers and had no intention of stopping. Moments later, the ball of gravity dragging me like a big dog dragging a child holding its leash impacted the hull of the freighter and the hull seemed to twist and warp before crumpling into the singularity, exposing sparking wiring and the innards of the ship.

I followed its trail of destruction and tried not to look too closely. Human casualties were a reality of war, but that didn't mean I had to see my enemies torn asunder by the intense gravitational waves and sucked into vacuum.

Within moments, the singularity and I were through the enemy ship and flashing through open space. I decreased the flow of power feeding the singularity and turned to look at my handiwork.

Two halves of the enemy ship floated listlessly through space, interacting in a strange dance as they twisted independent of one another. Debris, including, I had no doubt, human crew members, clustered like a cloud of gnats around the wreckage.

I swung the gravity ball around and pointed it to the side of the wrecked freighter, toward where flashes of light indicated remnants of the battle. I hoped they did not herald the death of the *Voltir* - they were my ride out of there. Increasing the flow of my power to the singularity and casting it further out, I shot through space once more.

Moments stretched into minutes as I realized just how far the *Voltir* had moved off-course. I noted two more fighter husks as I closed with it. Then, as I watched, a stream of coilgun shells followed by an explosion heralded the end of the final fighter.

I breathed a sigh of relief and headed toward the top of the *Voltir*.

The only problem was...the Voltir didn't stop. It continued accelerating through space as if it were still being pursued.

*Jarvis,* I thought to my implant. *Can you contact the* Voltir? I knew my implant could use communication arrays or towers to communicate medium distances but was the *Voltir* listening? My stomach sank.

*I am unable to establish a direct connection. However, I can broadcast the signal using my internal power core for a short distance.*

*How short?*

*A few hundred kilometers.*

*Shit.* In interstellar terms, that was a minuscule distance, and the *Voltir* was likely out of range already. *No other choice.* I could travel fast, and the vacuum of space did not affect me, but it would still take me years to reach the nearest system even at top speed. I could not travel, to my knowledge, even close to the speed of light.

I cast my singularity forward with a vengeance. How dare they leave me behind. I had to catch them.

The *Voltir's* captain knew I was pursuing him, for he jerked his ship this way and that, trying to throw me off the trail.

I would not be so easily shaken. With precision aiming, I directed the singularity to follow the *Voltir* and gained on them. I had to reach the ship before it made the shift to shadow space. Why they hadn't shifted yet was a mystery to me.

*Open the channel,* I directed to Jarvis. Then, without waiting for an acknowledgment, I began speaking in my mind, allowing Jarvis to convert my thoughts into a broadcast signal. *Attention starship* Voltir. *This is your security officer, Rachel, requesting permission to board.*

Several seconds passed and no response.

*I helped save your asses and* this *is how you thank me? Abandoning me to the void?*

"You are cursed," the captain's voice came through the link. "You are a demon and not welcome aboard the *Voltir.*"

*Bloody hell,* I thought before realizing my thoughts were still being broadcast. *How can you believe that? Open the top hatch and slow your ass down so I can board and then we can have a discussion.* I left off how the discussion would likely end with me kicking their asses.

"We will not comply. May the Seven have mercy upon your soul." The words had a sense of finality to them, but the ship continued on its path, showing no sign of shifting to shadow space or targeting me.

*Turn off my transmitter,* I commanded Jarvis. *Any speculation as to why the* Voltir *hasn't made the jump to shadow space yet?*

*Based upon my calculations, I believe the gravitational field emitted by the singularity you are bound to is preventing the* Voltir *from entering shadow space.*

*Like a magic nullification field?* I asked.

*No. Gravitational fields do not nullify the energy and mass manipulation abilities of mages. However, it is well-documented how strong gravitational fields prevent shifting nearby. Examples are planets, stars, black holes.*

*Then how can my cousin and aunt shift on bloody planets?*

*Current theory states that the negation field generated by an object with a strong gravity field is directly proportional to the mass of the object attempting to shift.*

*Meaning?* I hated it when my implant was cryptic. Yes, I'd been a physics student, but this was next-level stuff, and I was tired from the battle.

*Meaning small objects, such as humans, are unaffected by the gravity from planets and small stars while larger objects, such as starships, are affected by such sources.*

*Okay, that makes sense...kind of,* I thought. Quantum physics was my uncle's specialty. *So, my singularity is stopping the* Voltir *from entering shadow space.* An evil grin spread across my face. *Let's catch up and say hello.*

"Release us from your hold, Demon!" the captain shouted over the link.

*Reactivate my transmitter, Jarvis.* I waited until a mental beep indicated the transmitter was active. *Not until you let me in!* I replied, putting as much force as possible into my thoughts. *Your ship doesn't leave until you let me in.*

"We will fire upon you!" he declared.

I gestured behind me, though I knew the motion would not be seen by them. *Try it and you'll end up like the ships that were pursuing you. The ships I tore apart. I'll say again, let me in. You're not going anywhere until I come aboard.* I readied my gravity ball, preparing to launch it toward the *Voltir* and cruise through the ship I'd been hired to protect if they still refused to help me. *I can find my way back,* I thought, aware the statement was being transmitted as communication.

They fell silent for a long, long moment. So long I almost hurled the gravity ball and asked questions later.

"Fine. We will allow you to board the ship. But you will confine yourself to your quarters for the remainder of the journey."

*What if the ship is attacked again?*

"We should only be so lucky," the voice of the first mate came over the link.

*You have a deal*, I replied.

# Chapter 2

"Here's your pay," the captain said, handing me a credit chip. He made every possible effort to avoid my gaze.

I snatched it from his hand. "Thanks," I said, grudgingly. "You know," I started, mischievous grin forming, "I'm available for more work."

*That* got the captain to meet my eyes. "Demoness. You will never again set foot on my ship."

I sighed. "Of course not. Just remember who saved your ass from pirates."

"You probably summoned them, temptress," the first mate chimed in from several feet away.

"Come over here and say that to my face, or shut your mouth," I shot back. Such a notion was preposterous. It was even more preposterous that such backward notions as demons and the like had made their way among the stars. *There's a sucker born every minute,* I thought, remembering a phrase my father used to use. *My father.* The thought of him summoned his face, and with it the memories of events months ago. Maybe I was possessed by a demon - one who summoned painful memories at random times.

"Take the credits and go. And...thank you," the captain said, the last two words sounding as though he was being strangled as he spoke.

I pocketed the credit chip, flipped the first mate an inappropriate sign with my middle finger, and turned to leave the docking bay. The feeling of eyes on me caused me to look around.

Near the ship, half a dozen crew members from the *Voltir* glared at me, but it wasn't their attention that caused my hackles to rise. Near the exit of Dock 57 leaned a dark-haired, bulky, gruff man chewing on a cigar. His eyes never left me, even under the weight of my gaze. Polite people would avert their gaze.

I held his gaze for as long as I felt comfortable. Then, just before I looked away, I appealed to my implant. *Jarvis, can you take a picture of that man's face? He's creeping me out.*

*I can activate the eidetic memory module*, Jarvis informed me. *This will record any memories you experience until you ask me to stop or become unconscious next. Would you like me to activate it?*

*Activate it long enough to record that creeper. Then cross-reference him with the Federation database to see if we can identify who he is.*

*I regret to inform you that while I can record him, I do not have access to the Federation database any longer. I therefore cannot identify him.*

"Shit," I muttered aloud. Of course that was the case. *Do what you can.* I didn't want to face further reminders of how far I had fallen.

*Eidetic memory mode activated*, Jarvis informed me. I felt no difference. *Eidetic memory mode deactivated*, he continued, seconds later.

*Was that enough time?* I asked.

*Of course. It takes but a second to capture the memory. I delayed the deactivation so as not to jar you any more than necessary.*

*Gee, thanks*, I replied, half-injecting sarcasm into my thoughts. How nice of my implant to think of his poor underpowered human host.

*You are quite welcome*, Jarvis replied, either unaware of the sarcasm or choosing not to acknowledge it.

Having stared at the gruff stranger for long enough, I made for the exit, back straight and head up, eyes focused on the doorway next to the man.

I was within a few feet of the man, cigar smoke wafting into my nostrils, when I looked to him again, this time looking for more details. I considered reactivating eidetic memory mode but figured it would be redundant. I stopped next to him, eyes straight ahead once more. "Do you have a problem with me," I asked, putting as much Army Ranger into my voice as possible.

The man grunted and puffed a ring of smoke out of his cigar. "Watch yourself," he grumbled out one side of his mouth.

Irritated, I snapped my hand out and pinched the tip of his cigar with my fingers, extinguishing the flame. The heat washed up my fingers, but the pain vanished as soon as it came. Being undead had its perks. "Ask them," I tilted my head toward where the crew of the *Voltir* still stood, "what happens to those who get in my way."

Without waiting for a response, I stalked out of Docking Bay 57 and into the main terminal of Faltross Station.

A SHORT WHILE LATER, I sat at the bar, drink in my hand. I stared at the video feeds but didn't watch them. Sports were shallow and the talking heads of the news annoyed me. The events of the last few days played over and over in my head, adding to a storm of thoughts regarding events of the last few months. There'd been no contact from my father in a long time, not that I cared that much. I saw him on the news from time to time, but out here among the nonaligned planets, we didn't get much news about the Federation.

Once again, I felt eyes on the back of my head. I tried to surreptitiously look around. In the corner sat two men talking. One of the men looked sideways at me. I gave him a full-on glare, and he returned his attention to his cup.

Just then I felt a stab in my neck, a little poke, and I slapped at the spot. Moments later, my vision started to blur, and I looked around, frantically, trying to find the source of what I now knew was an attack.

*Foreign nerve agent detected,* Jarvis screeched, alarm bells blaring in my head. But his voice and the alarm faded as the drug took hold and blackness overtook me.

I AWOKE AN INDETERMINABLE time later. I was upright in a gloomy, cavernous room, my back pressed against something hard. I tried to move my arms but found my wrists and arms encased in metal restraints. My legs were similarly restrained, and I felt a cool metal encompassing my throat. I strained against my restraints, feeling my muscles bulge and the strange fluid inside my veins pumping. But even the enhanced strength of being undead was of no avail.

Despair mixed with panic flooded me at that moment. Images of me being surrounded by a mob of hateful people, being pummeled to a bloodied pulp and almost dying, watching my friend be ripped to shreds by the crowd flashed through my mind. I let out a hysterical, feral, scream of rage and frustration, as if those emotions alone would free me from these bonds.

*Snap out of it*, I said to myself. *You are a freaking Army Ranger. You've trained for situations like this. The drug must have disoriented you, that's all.* I was right, I knew I was, and I focused on my surrounding - on escape.

My eyes had adjusted to the gloom, and though I could not move my head very far, only a few inches from side to side, I could tell I was in a warehouse of some sort. Racks of metal crates towered on either side of me toward a cavernous ceiling, with a line of yellow or orange paint on the floor. I had to still be on Faltross Station, as it would be too hard for them to smuggle out an unconscious woman, wouldn't it?

I considered calling out for aid, but quickly dismissed the idea. Any help that I called would simply be in more danger. No one knew I was on the station, so no help would come from the Federation. *Wait. My implant. How could I have forgotten?*

*Jarvis,* I called out. *Can you hear me?*

Jarvis normally answered my queries instantly, so the two seconds it took him to reply felt painstakingly slow. Something was wrong. *I am here, ma'am,* he replied, his mechanical tone sounding inexplicably sluggish - as though he were drunk or drugged too.

*What happened?* I demanded. *I thought you were a military-grade implant. How did that drug incapacitate us?*

*Processing query.*

*Jarvis...* He'd never needed to think like this before.

*The drug used to incapacitate you was encased in a nanite-resistant micro-structure that allowed it to pass through your enhanced blood-brain barrier. Then, the micro-structure disintegrated, releasing an electric shock strong enough to disable me, which disabled the nanite defenses in your brain. The drug was then free to incapacitate you like a normal human.*

*Is that why you're talking so slow? The electric shock?*

*Yes. Some of my systems were damaged by the attack. I am attempting repairs.*

*How long will that take?*

*I do not have an estimate at this time.*

I gritted my teeth. *Okay. Let me know when you're back in full operation. We need a plan to get out of here. Can I use my powers?*

*I am afraid not. The collar around your neck is inhibiting all manipulation of matter and energy known to man. The only recorded case of the collar not functioning is concerning manipulation of space-time fields generated by your father.*

*Great, my father is immune to the collars?*

*According to the historical records, yes.*

*Better than me at everything,* I groused.

*Once you're fully operating, can you do anything about the collar?*

*I am afraid not. The nanites cannot exit your skin or they could disassemble the collar.*

*That's too bad. Make a note to tell my Uncle Jason to invent nanites that* can *do that.*

*Noted.*

*It was a...never mind.*

I turned my attention again to my industrial surroundings. I didn't know the layout of the station well enough to know where the warehouses were and had no inkling as to what the crates surrounding me contained.

Screeching metal behind me perked my ears up. It sounded like a door opening.

"Hello? Who's there?"

I kicked myself for being so naive a moment later. That's just what my captors would want, a nervous-sounding prisoner. They had to know about my powers if they used the collar meant to suppress energy-manipulating abilities and fit me with enough restraints to hold down twenty men. Did that mean they knew who I was? The second question was what did they want, and did I need to be alive for them to get it?

A man came into view just then, pale wrinkled face, dark hair, and wearing spectacles. He held a datapad. He tapped something into it and a row of lights above us activated, causing me to close my eyes against the light for a moment. When I opened them, I found him looking me up and down. I felt fortunate that I was still dressed, but the way he was leering made me doubt whether they would remain on much longer.

"So, you are the freak from the freighter," he said. "The one scaring all the crews."

Inwardly, I sighed in relief, forcing my face to show no emotion. He didn't know who I was. He thought I was a mercenary with special powers, which explained the restraints and collar. If he knew who I was, he might have already slit my throat and dumped my body into space. Or tried to ransom me to dear old dad.

"You caught me," I said. "I'm sorry I saved the crew of the *Voltir's* collective asses from certain demise. So why don't you just let me go before I do to you what I did to those pirate ships?"

The man laughed and pointed at my collar. "That collar will suppress your powers. There's no way for you to escape, no matter how powerful you are."

*Don't count me out yet*, I thought. No one had ever tried to suppress my powers using a collar, so there was a slight chance that my powers, like my father's powers, would work even with a collar on. I reached out with my mind to the part of me where my power resided but found nothing. Not the darkness that represented my gravity powers - just nothing. An absence of power. My connection to whatever power I had must have been severed. *Here I thought my power came from within me. Am I just a conduit?*

"Do you want revenge? Do you want money?" *Not that I have much money to give.* I'd been working on the *Voltir* for a reason.

"We want you to suffer," the man said. "But before that, we will have a little fun. "He withdrew a belt knife. It was long and looked very sharp. Then it started vibrating. *Great, a vibroblade.* Those things hurt like hell.

Somehow, despite my circumstances, I found the size of the blade humorous. "Are you trying to compensate for something?" I asked, using what little neck mobility the collar afforded me to nod toward his knife. "That's an awfully long knife."

The man, understanding at first, reddened as the realization of what I had said dawned on him. "You will find out soon enough," he said but made no move to use the knife on me.

"Well, let me just settle in and wait," I said. *I'm not scared,* I thought, reassuring myself. *I've been in tighter scrapes than this, and I've even died before.* If he wanted to kill me, so be it. I'd made my peace...sort of...with my father. I didn't *want* to die again, but the prospect no longer scared me.

"How did you come by your powers? The power to destroy those ships."

"I was born that way," I lied. He wouldn't believe me if I'd said it was a science experiment gone wrong. And that could lead to further questions about where the science experience had taken place, which could lead to my true identity becoming known.

"You are lying," he said. "But we will get the truth out of you. One way, or another. We have ways of making you talk."

"Bring it on," I said, my bravado in full swing. *Are you fully functional yet, Jarvis?* Nanites wouldn't help me escape, but they could ensure I endured immense amounts of pain and healed rapidly. Those, on top of the undead virus, would keep me going strong for a long time.

*Almost, ma'am. I estimate sixty seconds.*

The door screeched open again. "Now, now, Igor, you will scare our guest."

*Wait. Was Igor only a henchman? He looked like the main attraction.*

The new man came into view, this time touching my shoulder as he passed. He was blond-haired, blue-eyed and, I had to admit, more handsome than Igor. He wore no glasses, but his eyes were mismatched colors.

"You know why we took you?" He asked

"To punish me for something," I said. "Did the captain of that ship send you? He didn't like that I saved his ass?"

"On the contrary, my dear, I'm sure the captain is quite grateful, though he will not long enjoy the fruit of your labor. No, I'm here on behalf of the ships you destroyed."

*Nanites are fully functional, ma'am.*

*Thanks. I'll probably need them.* I gulped as the implication of the man's words set in. They weren't mad that I'd saved the freighter, they were mad that I destroyed several of their ships in the process of saving it.

"So where does that leave us?" I asked.

"It leaves us asking questions," the man said, in a lazy tone. "But, if you tell us what we want to know, we might let you live."

"I don't know much, just ask my teachers at school." That wasn't quite a lie. My history professor *had* told me that, even if the others would have disagreed.

"You think you're so clever," the man said, "but you are not. Have no fear, for we will make you understand, soon enough."

I met his eyes, putting as much challenge into them as possible, while I envisioned ripping out his spine in my mind. "Do your worst," I said punctuating each word.

# Chapter 3

Several hours later, I stood half-naked, chained to the ceiling, as Igor whipped me with chains and sliced me with his long knife. My nanites, combined with my undead healing properties, meant I healed quickly. The downside to that was he tortured me more often. The second man had forbidden him from going further than torturing me, so far anyway, for which I was grateful.

Though my mind had begun to drift as they tortured me, in a particularly lucid moment I reached out to my implant. *Jarvis, is there any way you can send out a call for help?*

*There is a heavy jamming present in this room. Due to my military-grade construction, I can break through, but only on a military frequency.*

*Is that a bad thing?*

*If there are no Federation military vessels or operatives in range, yes.*

*Oh. Well, send it anyway. It's better than doing nothing.* The last thing I wanted was my father coming to my rescue, but that was better than dying again.

*Acknowledged. Sending signal.*

My mind went back to drifting as the torture resumed. I drifted first to my childhood and then to my time as an Army Ranger and back to the plaza where I was assaulted. I had faced worse, I told myself. There is nothing they can do to me that hadn't been done before. Was I right? Or would they break me?

DAYS HAD PASSED, UNCOUNTED days unless I asked Jarvis for a count, with no help, no aid, not even an acknowledgment of my message. Igor would torture me until the floor was covered in blood and I was on the brink of second death. Then he would relent, for a brief respite, allowing my wounds to close. Then he would return and do it all again.

I continued to strain, attempting to reach my powers, but it was no use, the collar had effectively blocked my powers.

I never told them anything, not about my life before, or about my origins. I didn't even have a rank or serial number to repeat and dared not give my real name. So I stood in silence. Still they asked, wanting to know the secret behind the woman who destroyed so many of their ships. I couldn't tell if it was out of revenge or curiosity. Did they want to break me so they could turn me into their weapon, or did they want to break me so they could kill me at the end? In either case, I resolved they would not succeed.

It was always Igor who tortured me, and the second, unnamed man, referred to only as "sir" by Igor, would come in to bring me a sandwich or drink, to sit with me during my brief respites. I knew the good cop bad cop routine would not work on me, but still, I couldn't help but feel some sense of trust with the second man, before feeling betrayed by my mind, and my feelings. *He's not your friend, idiot. He's the enemy and wants the same thing Igor wants - whatever that is.*

"Just tell us how you really came to have your powers," the blond man asked. "That's all we want to know."

I laughed while chewing a ham sandwich he'd held up to my mouth moments before and broke my no-speaking rule for the first time in days. "If you think I believe that, do you have a bridge to sell me on a desert world too? I know you just want me dead."

"No, not at all," he said in his smooth voice. "We want to use you, yes, but we don't want you dead right now, or you already would be. On the contrary, we want to make you our partner."

*Partner. They have a twisted way of recruiting partners.* "I..."

An explosion shook the room. It sounded like it was outside the room behind me, but I couldn't tell for sure. All thoughts of giving the man a piece of my mind fled.

The blond man stood up and drew a pistol from his belt. "Stay here," he said, before racing out of the room and slamming the door behind him and leaving me alone.

In the distance a secondary set of explosions echoed, then I heard the distinctive pop pop pop of coil guns being fired. Even though the weapons were dangerous to use on a space station and starships, they were often used by mercenaries who had no access to laser weaponry or who preferred to see bullets piercing their victims instead of lasers burning. Also, it was hard to protect against coil gun shells, considering that they were magnetically propelled and it was difficult to absorb all the kinetic energy from them. A laser could be nullified by armor much easier than a bullet.

Had someone heard my message? Had help arrived? Or was it merely a coincidence? Were the people who kidnapped me winning? Judging by the panicked pace of the blond man, I would guess that they were losing, but I didn't dare get my hopes up.

Several minutes later, after the sound of gunfire had died down, I heard the door creak open one more time. "We found someone," a filtered voice, like one of someone wearing a helmet, said. It sounded male, but voices could be deceiving when wearing a helmet.

A set of boots clanked on the floor as a figure passed me. They made no move to touch me, just looked me up and down, and then looked around the room. "Are you alone?"

I felt grateful at that moment that I wasn't hanging half-naked on the wall again waiting to be lashed or beaten. They'd dressed me in a stinky brown shirt before feeding me "Yes," I replied. "There was a blond man who was interrogating me, and he left through that door," I threw my head back to indicate the door behind me. "You mind unshackling me?"

"Of course. Where are my manners?" They hit a button on their arm controls and their helmet visor retracted, revealing a male face. He was young, looking to be in his 20s, with brown hair and blue eyes. He wore black combat armor, along with all the accrued accouterments of a soldier. But his armor bore no emblem, and it did not look like standard Federation issue armor. "Are you from the Federation?" I asked.

He hesitated, then shook his head. "No, I'm a mercenary and I was hired to do a job."

"The job involves saving me?" I asked

"No," the man said matter-of-factly. "We were hired to clear up this den of pirates. We weren't expecting to find you. Who are you?" His gaze shifted to the collar at my neck and the restraints on my arms and legs. "That's an awful lot of the restraints for a young woman like you."

*Young woman? He's one to talk. He looks barely older than me.* "There's more to me than meets the eye," I said. How much did I dare tell this mercenary? On the one hand, he did save my life, but on the other, he was likely in it for the money, feigning care about me in the hopes of getting a fat paycheck out of the deal.

He chuckled, then stood. "Let's get you out of these restraints, and then head back to the ship."

"You have a ship?" I asked

"Sure do. It's called the *Dauntless*, and it's a lot safer than staying here."

"You think more of his goons will show up?"

The man shrugged. "It stands to reason they will eventually. Or someone worse."

"Lead the way," I said, then tried to move my arms. "Right after you get me out of these things."

He flashed a roguish grin at me, then proceeded to deactivate all of the controls for the restraints. When he got to the collar, he muttered something under his breath and looked up into my eyes. "I thought that looked familiar. Are you a mage?"

"Not exactly," I said. "I have...powers...that allow me to manipulate gravity with my mind."

His eyes widened. "Nice! How did you get those?"

"Freak accident," I said.

He held my gaze for a few moments, then opened his mouth and closed it. He nodded. "Okay."

*He doesn't believe me,* I thought. That fact, at least, was the truth.

He unlocked the collar, somehow, and I felt my powers return to me at full force. I flexed with my mind and created a small gravity well far above our heads, just for show. A few crates wobbled.

The man looked up and nodded approvingly. "Neat trick." Then he held out his hand, palm upward, and summoned a flame. It floated above his hands, like an ethereal ghost of red and orange.

It was my turn to be surprised. "You're a mage?"

He smirked, and the flame disappeared. "Yup, I have been for a long time."

*Time to call his bluff.* "You can't be any older than 25. So you mean since birth?"

"Yeah, something like that." He winked.

I stepped out of the now unlocked restraints and took a couple of hesitant steps, then stretched. "Oh, that feels good."

"How long were you in here? And is all that yours?" he gestured to the blood soaking the floor.

"Several days. And yes, that's all mine. I heal fast." I gestured toward the door. "Lead the way."

"I'm Michael, by the way," he said.

"I am... Reina," I said, catching myself. He had the look and feel of a Federation Marine, or special forces, even if he didn't wear the Federation insignia. I continued to be wary of identifying myself to him even with my real first name.

"Cute name, I like it."

"You would've said that regardless of the name I gave you, wouldn't you?"

"I guess we'll never know," he said, again with that smirk. A handsome smirk, but kind of annoying.

He led me out of the warehouse and into a control building. We passed the bodies of several of my captors, including Igor, who stared up through broken glasses with a vacant gaze. He would never again torture anyone as he tortured me. I fought the urge to kick him, punch him, or destroy him with gravity. But he'd already received the greatest punishment, and he was beyond my reach now.

The blond man, however, was nowhere to be found. I still hadn't learned his name.

Michael led me to what looked like a dirty mess hall. More corpses were here, shot where they'd sat. "You had the element of surprise," I observed. My gaze flicked to three other figures in armor dragging corpses into a pile and looting them.

"Sure did," one of the figures said, straightening. "What happened to you?" he retracted his helmet visor, revealing a lanky man with a pocked face.

"A lot," I said, holding back what I wanted to say. *I was tortured for days on end, that's what*. But there wasn't time for that. Sub-consciously I looked down at what little clothing I wore. "Do you have something I can wear? This shirt stinks." I asked Michael.

"Sure thing. Maggie, you're her size," he pointed to another mercenary who was kneeling next to a corpse. "Let her have your suit until we get back to the *Renegade*."

"Whatever you say, Captain," Maggie said. She stood and hit a button on her suit. Her helmet and suit retracted into a single chest piece held on by straps. She undid the straps and hefted it. "Catch." She tossed it unceremoniously and I snagged it out of the air.

*They have Federation tech*, I thought. We'd had similar in spec ops. Most mercenaries had armor that went on in plates and sealed together over a bodysuit. The nano-suits were newer tech and distribution was still controlled by the Federation. *He must have connections within the Federation.* My feelings of the need for secrecy intensified.

Maggie watched me with green eyes, then nodded. "Ignore Reynaldo. He can be a bit blunt sometimes."

"Like a hammer to the head," the third figure said. He too retracted his visor, then bowed overly deep. "Unlike me. The name's Frank."

Maggie just rolled her eyes and got back to what she was doing, dark-skinned hands rummaging through one of the pirates' rucksack.

"Are all the bodies gathered?" Michael asked. "I just passed one in the hall."

"Let me get that, boss man," Frank said, giving a mock salute and jogging past us. He flashed me a roguish smile as he passed.

"Is it just the three of you?" I asked while we waited.

"Yes. I hired these three and supplied the ship."

"I'm impressed that you managed to kill..." I did a quick sweep of the room with my eyes and tallied the bodies, "...over a dozen pirates with no casualties of your own."

"It was nighttime, for one," Michael said.

"And they were all here stuffing their faces," Reynaldo said.

"And they were inept," Maggie added.

"I got the last one," Frank announced, carrying in Igor. "Gravedigger duties are done."

"I don't see any graves, so you're not a gravedigger," Michael said. He stared at the bodies for a long moment. "I could incinerate them or leave them for the authorities. What do you guys think?"

If you leave them for the authorities," Maggie began, "their associates might hear about it and come looking for us."

"That's what I want," Michael said.

I looked at him as if he were crazy. "Are you out of your mind? You *want* to bring the wrath of more pirates on us?"

"Why do you think we raided this warehouse?" He asked.

*Not to rescue me, we established that.* "You said you were hired to raid a pirate den. I assumed that meant clear it out *quietly*."

Michael shook his head. "I've been chasing this group of pirates for a long time, and this group had the information I needed. I'm looking for the main base, and I think that leaving the bodies out that may draw their associates into the open sooner, rather than later. It can't be a trap if they know about it."

"I wouldn't be so sure," I grumbled. "You know what they say about the best-laid plans of mice and men."

"Yeah, I do."

"Well I don't," Reynaldo announced. "What's it mean?"

Michael kept his eyes on me. "It means that even our best-laid plans will sometimes go awry, he said."

"Always go awry," I said, correcting him.

"Well, we'll see what happens, won't we?"

I held his gaze. His blue eyes were entrancing. "I guess so."

"Everybody back aboard the dauntless," he said. "Maggie, trigger the distress call please."

"On it, Captain."

"Do you need to collect any belongings before we go?" Michael asked me.

I snorted. "No. I am...was...a drifter. I hadn't settled in here and didn't anything with me other than my clothes and sidearm, which I assume you can provide me with more of."

He nodded. "Want to come along with us, then?"

"And get payback on the monsters behind my abduction?" The face of the blond man flashed in my mind's eye. I wouldn't forget *that* face. "Of course."

Michael extended a hand. "Welcome aboard."

# Chapter 4

We entered the docking bay of Faltross Station and I gasped. The *Renegade* looked like a modified Federation gunship, further solidifying my thoughts that there was more to Michael than met the eye. A dual-barrel cannon sat on the top and another hung from the bottom, while the ship itself was rectangular with two barrels sticking from the front and what looked like a missile launcher on each side of the cockpit.

"That's some ship," I said. "Isn't it a little cozy inside, though?" Those types of gunships were typically attached to capital ships and used for tactical insertion, not long-distance space travel.

Michael smiled. "It's heavily modified. Come on."

The ramp to the gunship lowered as we approached, and the three other mercenaries went aboard.

Michael hung back and gestured toward the ramp. "After you."

Inside the ship, I found a table with a bench, presumably where the crew lounged while not fighting or doing whatever mercenaries did. "Nice common area. I didn't know this model of ship had this much space."

"A small concession," Michael admitted. "This is larger than Federation tactical gunships. It's custom-built and suited for deep space travel and long missions."

*He must have a lot of pull to get a custom military-style ship built.* "I'd love to see the weapon complement."

"There'll be time for that later. Up there is the cockpit," he pointed to a ramp straight ahead. "Crew quarters are down those hallways," he gestured to two parallel openings leading out of the rec room. "Engineering is that way," he pointed to a doorway to the right. "Making it two stories was one of the concessions I was talking about."

"I can see that." I had to admit, it was impressive.

"Yours will be down that hall," he pointed to the hallway ahead of us and to the right. "Room five."

"How many rooms are aboard this ship?"

"Six crew quarters. Two of them can double as a brig if needed, and the sixth room currently is."

"You have someone in there?"

"No. But it's standing ready."

"Ah. Can I see the cockpit?"

"Of course."

He led me up the ramp and past a ladder that I assumed went to the top and bottom gun batteries. On the right was the door to an airlock, space suits hung neatly on the wall.

"Is this her maiden voyage?" I asked. "She seems too organized to be a seasoned ship."

"Close. We've only been together for a few weeks. Hit some other pirate dens, but this was the biggest haul hit yet."

"Impressive," I said idly as we approached the door to the cockpit.

The room was a semi-circle, with a wide viewport showing the stars outside. Inside, I found Frank performing a pre-flight check on the *Renegade*. Reynaldo sat at his side assisting.

"Frank is our pilot," Michael explained. "Reynaldo is the navigator and fills the role of gunner during battle."

"And the co-pilot in a pinch," he put in.

"Maggie is our engineer. She spends most of her time at the aft of the ship."

"Fixing what we break," Frank put in.

"And we break a lot," Reynaldo said.

"And what do you do?" I asked, looking to Michael. "Eat bon-bons?"

For the first time since meeting him, Michael looked embarrassed. "I'm the captain, but I usually act as the co-pilot. I'm not the pilot of my family."

"So, you have siblings?" *Don't be so familiar,* I scolded myself. *You just met the guy.*

"A twin sister," he said. "She's a hotshot pilot. I don't see her often."

"That's nice." *A hotshot pilot in the Federation perhaps?*

"Shall we go talk in the common area? Or do you want to see your quarters first?"

"Quarters, then talk. In the common area. Not in my quarters." I would have blushed if I was capable of doing so.

He smiled knowingly. "Follow me." He led me back through the common area and down the hallway containing my quarters. A quick swipe over the door control caused the door to slide up. "It'll be keyed to your wrist control and biometrics."

The room was functional, with a bunk with basic sheets, a sink, and a refresher. There were no display screens in the room. "It'll do," I said.

Right then, Maggie entered the room. "I have clothes that should fit you." She set them on my bunk.

"And you want your armor back," I observed.

"I have an extra suit that can be yours," Michael assured me.

"Okay. Will you two leave me in peace while I get changed?"

Michael bowed. "I'll await your presence in the common area." He and Maggie left, and the door slid closed behind them.

I sighed. *Jarvis, can you check for listening devices?*

*I am detecting no radio or other wireless signals in this room.*

*Good.* Not that I'd expected there to be any - they hadn't even known I was arriving. Still, there could be hidden video surveillance equipment watching me. I wouldn't be able to completely let my hair down.

I removed the armor Maggie lent me and removed the remains of the brown shirt the pirates had dressed me in. Then I hit the refresher and let the warm water run down my body, washing away the dirt, grime, and dried blood-that-wasn't-blood I'd acquired during my time of captivity. Then, feeling clean, I donned new clothing and carried the armor and scraps of clothing out into the common area.

Michael and Maggie were talking in low tones when I entered and stopped when they noticed me. Maggie approached, took her armor from my arms, and headed straight toward engineering.

"Don't mind her. She's distrustful of newcomers."

"I don't blame her," I admitted. I hefted my ruined clothing. "Do you have a refuse bin?"

He eyed the scraps. "For those? No, just set them on the floor."

I raised an eyebrow. "The floor?"

He nodded insistently.

I did as he asked.

"Step back please."

When I'd taken two steps back, Michael gazed at the clothing and they erupted in flame.

"Whoa!" I said, looking from the ashes of my bloody clothing to Michael. "I forgot you were a mage. Are the others...?"

"Mundanes. I was the only one with magic...until you came along."

*Please don't ask more questions about my powers,* I thought desperately. "So, tell me about this pirate group and why you're hunting them."

"All in good time," he smirked. "First, let's depart. I didn't want to jar you with our departure as you were changing, but we have places to be."

"I'm not fragile," I replied, injecting steel into my voice.

"I didn't think you were. Just common courtesy."

"Oh." It had been a while since I'd met a courteous man. *Have I forgotten what it means to be civilized?*

"Frank," Michael called up the ramp. "Take us out!"

"You got it, Boss," Frank called back.

The ship jolted as the *Renegade* rose from its moorings and moved out of the docking bay. There were no viewports here, but I felt the artificial gravity of the station cease affecting the ship as we momentarily floated weightlessly. But a heartbeat later the gravity generator aboard the *Renegade* engaged and gravity returned, wrapping me in its embrace. Ever since my gravity powers had emerged, I felt the fluxes of gravity more acutely than at any time in my life.

"Now," Michael began, "I think there's an elephant in the room."

"Oh?" I braced myself, waiting for him to guess my identity. *Here it comes.*

"I noticed your pale complexion...and your intermittent breathing, and the odd-looking blood back on the station from where you were tortured. And this question would have been ludicrous three years ago but..."

"Yes, I'm undead," I said. "I'll spare you the words. I was on Galatia IV when the outbreak occurred. I got infected, died, and rose again."

"That must have been hard. I'm sorry."

"You have nothing to be sorry about," I said.

"And then you joined the military?"

"How did you guess?"

"The way you carry yourself. Infantry?"

"Something like that," I hedged. "I know my way around a rifle."

"Good. We'll need your rifle for the fights to come."

"Who exactly are we fighting and why?"

Michael took a deep breath before speaking. "They're called the Crimson Marauders."

"How unoriginal," I said dryly.

"The name might be boring, but their intentions are anything but. They are a major criminal organization that calls the non-aligned planets their home. They organize raids into Federation territory, rape, pillage, and murder, and then flee back to safety. They've become a significant nuisance to the Federation - hence I was dispatched."

"Wait. So you *are* in the Federation?"

"Keep your voice down," he scolded. "The others don't know. But yes."

"Which branch?"

"Army, for now. I'm an officer, which is why I was chosen for this mission."

"So why did you assemble a crew of mercenaries instead of bringing along Federation Marines or soldiers?"

"This is an unofficial mission, which is why my true affiliation has to remain a secret. If it becomes known that the Federation is operating covert missions in non-aligned space the governments of many planets will be irate, which could have significant political ramifications."

"So why entrust me with the knowledge?"

He shrugged. "You said yourself you served. I'm guessing you already had inklings as to where my affiliations lay."

"Guilty as charged," I admitted. My eyes narrowed. "Are you supposed to bring down the entire Crimson Marauder organization with a single ship and three mercenaries?"

"I know it sounds crazy but bear with me. We're meant to follow the breadcrumbs as covertly as possible until we find the Crimson Marauders main base of operations. Then we call in the big guns and some nondescript Federation destroyers shift in to end the threat. In and out, a surgical strike."

I doubted the plan would go that smoothly, but I smiled indulgently. "Dead pirates sound good to me. Where to first?"

"The planet of Zignion V. It's a jungle planet rumored to hide a Crimson Marauder listening post."

"They have listening posts? Why?"

"They don't have enough ships to canvas large amount of area, so they use listening posts to eavesdrop on communications and relay it to nearby ships."

"And it keeps them decentralized," I noted. "Clever."

"That too," Michael confirmed. "Some of the governments in the non-aligned Planets have tried to exterminate their organization, with little success. Then the Marauders get revenge."

"Revenge?"

"Kidnapping family members of high-ranking officials, assassinations, uprisings. Fifty years they've been on the Federation's radar and they've left a trail of chaos in their wake. They're second only to the Cult of Rae in their threat level among organized crime organizations."

"You left out the Commerce Sector." I smirked.

He looked at me for a moment, deadpan, then burst out laughing. "Good one. Yes, they are the biggest crooks in the galaxy - only they're legal. Maybe one day they'll get what's coming to them."

I sobered. "So that's why the Federation is sending such a small team, isn't it? Plausible deniability."

"I hope they wouldn't disavow us," Michael replied, "but yes, they will claim no knowledge of our mission if we fail. Once we find the head of the snake, they'll come in to swing the sword. Until then, we're alone in the tall grass."

"The desert," I said.

"Hmm?"

"Alone in the desert," I explained. "There are more snakes in the desert."

"Depends on what planet you visit," he replied, then smirked.

"Prepare for the shift," Frank announced over the loudspeaker.

I buckled in and waited while Michael did the same. Restraints were recommended when shifting between the realms. Some said it was a superstitious habit left over from the pioneer days of interstellar travel, when it was believed physically connecting yourself to the ship would increase your chances of successfully shifting along with the ship. Or more accurately, decreasing your chances of being left behind. Of course, that was later shown to be nonsense, as my physics professor liked to point out at least twice a week, but the habit continued.

The ship jolted and lights briefly flickered as the shadow drive engaged. While less efficient than using a shadow walker, like Isabelle or my Aunt Bridgette, shadow drives had been the innovation that history recorded as the dawn of interstellar travel. Instead of a few hundred ships sailing through the cold dark, uncounted thousands departed Tar Ebon without the need of a human mind to transition between the real realm and the shadow realm.

*All thanks to Uncle Jason,* I thought. Centuries later and he was still regarded as the foremost genius in the Federation. I didn't know if I would see him again, but he was probably the only family member I didn't hate at the moment.

The ship hull turned transparent for a brief moment before solidifying once more. A trick of the mind or actual destabilization of matter? Physics didn't have an answer yet.

"Shift complete," Frank announced.

Michael and I both unbuckled.

I smiled at him. "If you don't mind, I'm going to hit the sack until we get there."

"Sounds good," he smiled in return. "We're just over six hours from our destination."

I walked to my room and the door slid open without incident. *Jarvis, please set an alarm for five hours and forty-five minutes. I want to be prepared before we shift out.*

*Of course, ma'am,* Jarvis replied dutifully as I lay down for sleep. Thankfully it was fast in coming.

# Chapter 5

The ship jolted and the light in my quarters dimmed briefly as the *Renegade* shifted back to real space. I rose from my bunk, where I had been lying awake for the past fifteen minutes, and made my way to the cockpit.

Michael was already there, looking like he too had gotten some sleep. He smiled as I entered the room. "Behold, Zignion V," then he gestured in a grandiose way as if presenting some great gift.

I rolled my eyes and followed his arms to view our target planet. It was a big ball of green floating in the void of space. What made it stand out from the thousands of other inhabited planets in the civilized section of the galaxy was the fact I saw *no* space stations orbiting the planet. That was almost unheard of in this era, especially for what looked like a luscious planet.

"What's the plan?" Reynaldo asked from the co-pilot seat.

Michael took a seat behind Frank and gestured to the seat behind Reynaldo. "We find the pirate facility, break in, and find some people to interrogate or gather intel. That means we need at least one *living* pirate. Hear that, Maggie?"

"I hear ya, boss," she said over the intercom. "Don't frag all the pirates before we get the information we need."

No hails or challenges came as we approached the planet, a fact that was not lost on Frank. "It's quiet. Too quiet."

"Are there *any* signals?" Michael asked.

"Some are coming from satellites," Reynaldo said. "I'm guessing that's the listening devices that relay signals down to the planet."

"Can you determine where all the signals are heading to?"

"Trying..." he began, punching a bunch of buttons on the controls and swiping. "They're routing through several layers of atmospheric satellites and bouncing the signals around, but I think I got a general location," he announced after several seconds. An image appeared on the overhead display, a red dot in a sea of green.

"Enter the atmosphere far away and skim the tree line until we're a few kilometers out. They may have spotted us, but they may not know that we're anything more than smugglers or private citizens going about our business. If we make straight for them, they'll be spooked."

"With respect, sir, I wasn't born yesterday," Frank said. "That was my plan."

"Coulda fooled me," Reynaldo said.

"Shut up and give me a travel solution, *navigator*."

A yellow circle overlaid the display of the planet and then a yellow line streaked toward the planet and slithered along the surface, weaving back and forth.

"Why the back-and-forth path?" I asked.

"Easier to avoid surface-to-air weapons," Frank said. "If they *do* spot us or suspect we're headed for them, they might preemptively launch ballistic missiles into our calculated path to make us go boom." He emphasized the "boom" with his hands expanding and produced sound effects too.

"Not going boom is a good thing," Reynaldo pointed out.

"Obviously," I said, smirking. Reynaldo had a way of stating the obvious. Or maybe I was being dense. I shrugged in my seat.

The flight of the *Renegade* continued without incident as we approached the atmosphere. I saw more satellites with the naked eye as we closed with the blue halo representing atmosphere, then we were through and the hull heated up as we entered, though the climate control compensated after a few warm moments. Once through, Frank began his jinking and juking pattern laid out by Reynaldo.

The *Renegade* skimmed over the tree line. The vegetation reminded me of any number of inhabited worlds in the Federation. Surprisingly, very few planets located within a certain distance from the star of their solar system had needed terraforming, a fact that was not lost on scientists...or conspiracy theorists. Theories of an omnipotent being populating the galaxy with habitations compatible with human life circulated within religious circles, something I had never subscribed to, especially after learning who my father was.

"Closing on target," Reynaldo announced. "Frank, I'm marking the landing spot."

"I'm not blind," Frank said, but complied a moment later and slowed the *Renegade.*

A few minutes later, we had touched down in a clearing surrounded by giant trees, which Jarvis identified as oak. I rose and stretched, then headed for the rear of the ship. Maggie met me there, already geared up, and the footsteps of the three men neared.

"I left a suit of armor in your room," Maggie said, again seeming to size me up with her eyes. "Should fit."

"Thanks," I said briskly before jogging to my cabin. Time was of the essence, as our presence could become known at any minute. If this had been a true military op we would have already been geared up before landing. *They're not exactly professionals, are they?* The adage "you get what you pay for" came to mind.

"How's it fit?" Maggie asked, after I'd donned my armor and returned to the common area. Surprisingly, I was the first one there.

"It'll do," I said, keeping my voice neutral. Maggie already had some unspoken beef with me, I didn't want to give her any more reasons. *It's not military-grade, or nanite-infused, like hers, but it'll do.* My nanite augments and powers would more than make up for any lack of sophistication in the armor.

Maggie sniffed. *Great. She read into* that.

Before I could say anything to her to get to the bottom of her distaste, Michael chose that moment to exit from his hallway. His gaze flicked to her and he raised an eyebrow. "Faster than me. Surprising."

"Lots of practice," I replied through the helmet commlink, smirking. *And super-human speed doesn't hurt.*

We stood in awkward silence for several moments before Reynaldo and Frank arrived almost in tandem from opposite hallways.

"Nice of the divas to join us," Michael teased. He slapped the door control and the rear hatch opened and the gangway extended. "Move out."

*There's the voice of command I'm used to,* I thought. I'd been good at following orders as a soldier...sometimes too good.

Twenty minutes of trudging through dense overgrowth later we came upon the outskirts of the pirate base. "Is that..."

"...an old temple," Michael finished. "Seems like it. And that," he pointed to a tower sticking out of the top of the temple," is how they're receiving the signals from the satellites."

"What, are the Crimson Marauders communing with their god?" Frank asked.

"They're going to be communing with the god of Death before we're done with them," Maggie said. "You know something about that, don't you Reina?"

I stared at her and frowned. Was that what her grudge against me was? "I certainly didn't meet any gods," I said. "I don't remember anything from being dead."

"Sounds like the afterlife is a bunch of bullshit then," Reynaldo declared.

"Maybe the undead go to a different place," Maggie said. "A place of eternal darkness and torment."

I opened my mouth to deliver a snappy retort...

"All right you two, cut the chatter," Michael cut in. "We've got a mission to do. Maggie, what kind of defenses can we expect?"

Maggie stood still as a statue, her face unreadable behind her tactical helmet. "One way in, one way out, unless you use heavy explosives, but you'd need a *lot* of explosives to blow through those walls. Each temple was custom-built, so the layout is unpredictable."

"Nice place to spring an ambush," Reynaldo chimed in.

"They don't know we're here yet, idiot," Frank said.

"Don't underestimate them just because they're pirates," Michael cautioned. "Many a Federation strike force or fleet has met their peril because of their hubris."

"What's hubris mean?" Reynaldo said.

"They got cocky," I summarized.

"Oh," the navigator said.

"So, let's be careful," Michael iterated. "How long until nightfall?"

"Too long," Maggie said.

"All right, let's hit them fast and hard." He suited action to words, crouched, and moved forward.

I and the others followed, rifles held at the ready should any marauders spring out of the entrance or surrounding forest.

Fortunately, no one popped out and we didn't come under fire. We stood on either side of the temple entrance and waited while Michael peeked around the corner. "Clear," he said, before moving around the corner.

A long, dark tunnel unbroken by any sign of security sensors led into the heart of the temple. A faint blue light glowed at the end and the tunnel opened into a large circular room.

"Let's split..." Michael's words were cut off by the boom of a coilgun. Stone shards exploded from the wall to his right. "Contact, contact!" he shouted, diving for cover behind a collapsed pillar.

Maggie and Frank emerged next and rushed to Michael's side, while Reynaldo and I went left to stand behind an upright pillar.

"Where are they shooting from?" I shouted as more shells whipped past or slammed into the pillar, causing a cloud of dust to swirl up.

"Up top, I think" Michael shouted. "Downward angle."

*Right, of course,* I thought, wanting to slap my head. Had I been away from being a soldier so long I'd forgotten how to track the trajectory of incoming bullets?

"I'll take care of this," I announced.

"Wait," Michael ordered. "That's an order."

Ignoring him, I drew upon my power and created a gravity shield. "Be ready to shoot while I draw their fire," I said. Then I stepped from behind the pillar.

A hail of bullets soared toward me, fast even to my enhanced reflexes...and disappeared into the singularity I'd projected, their potential and kinetic energy feeding the pool of darkness acting as my defense mechanism.

*I'm unstoppable*, I thought. It had been a while since I'd used my powers planet-side. *This is what I would have done if they hadn't stuck that damn collar around my neck back on the station.* Without waiting for more waves of bullets, I lifted into the air and sought my first target. I found him, moments later, firing from a hidden window high above the ground. I shot forward like an arrow, absorbing another string of bullets, and slammed into his firing position. The blow sent him flying back like a ragdoll, limbs flying in directions they weren't meant to go, and shook the temple. I floated back, unharmed, and sought my second target.

"Raina!" Michael shouted over the squad commlink, as his voice would have been too faint from where he hunkered behind a fallen pillar. "Remember our mission. We need them alive."

I refused to answer, the anger rising within me. I would never again be powerless. "Just a few more," I replied before cutting the link. I'd found my next target. This one stood in a similar opening on the right side of the temple but was smarter and tried jumping from the perch as

I soared toward him. "You won't get away that easily," I growled aloud, then halted him mid-fall and lifted him to float before me. I clapped my hands out in front of me. "Die," I said, dragging out the word before I spread my arms wide and ripped him in two with competing tidal forces.

"Raina!" Michael shouted again. "Stand down. That's an order."

"We're not in the military," I shot back. Without waiting for a retort, I drew upon more power and focused it into a ball in front of me. "And they deserve this." I hurled the ball into the air and toward the distant top of the temple. The temple shook as the top of the temple dissolved into the gravity well I'd produced.

"Go, go go," Michael shouted, this time not for me but the others. I saw them scurry out of the temple out of the corner of my eye.

I fed more power to the gravity well and the shaking intensified as the walls seemed to melt and swirl toward the void. In the daylight streaming through the wreckage, I saw bodies caught up in the storm of stone before disappearing into the darkness high above. Finally, mere minutes after I began my attack, the temple lay leveled at my feet. *I have my vengeance*, I thought.

Then I dropped and the darkness of unconsciousness took me.

I AWOKE SOMETIME LATER and looked around. The room looked like my quarters aboard the *Renegade*, but when I tried to sit up my arms were restrained.

Anger rose in me and I reached for my power.

"Before you release your wrath on yet another thing today," Michael spoke from behind me, "hear me out."

"You threw me in the brig?" I asked, realization dawning. "Did you knock me out too?"

"Yes, and yes," he said matter-of-factually as he came into view and pulled up a chair next to my bunk. "You were becoming unstable and a danger to my crew."

"If I'm so dangerous, why did you bring me back aboard?"

"Because we're not enemies, and we don't leave a soldier behind."

"I'm not a soldier. Not…"

"…not anymore, I know." He sighed. "By rights, I should boot you off my ship. Insubordination would get you court-martialed back in the Federation, and you'd go away for a long time. But," he held up a finger to forestall my next rebuttal, "we're not in the Federation, and, depending on how this conversation goes, I'm willing to give you another shot."

I focused my gaze on a speck of dirt on the floor. "I…" *Come on, Rachel, swallow your pride and say it,* I chastised myself. "…am sorry for deviating from the plan and disobeying your instructions."

Michael nodded. "Do you want to talk about it?"

*Not really.* "In the heat of the moment, I…felt restrained again. Helpless."

"Even though you were anything but helpless," Michael pointed out. "You were the most powerful person in the room. But being the most powerful person isn't always enough. Trust me, I know."

"Speaking from experience?"

"Yes. Being a mage in the military I saw a lot of prejudice against mages first-hand. Regular soldiers either treat you like you're a god or spoiled and snobbish. Both attitudes are not conducive to working as a team."

"So how did you overcome it?" I asked.

He leaned back in his chair. "I had to learn humility. I realized I was often acting as a one-man army, and not relying on my non-magical comrades to support me. After a few too many tough lessons, I finally learned, and my squad was better for it."

I chuckled. "So, you're saying I should be humbler, is that it?"

He cracked a smile. "That's exactly what I'm saying. Do you think you can do that?"

"I think so. Do you think they," I tilted my head to indicate the other three members of the *Renegade,* "will forgive me so easily?"

"Oh, I haven't forgiven you yet. I'm giving you a second chance, but I'll be keeping an eye on you." He added levity to his comment by pointing two fingers at his eyes and then one at me in the "I'm watching you" gesture and smiling.

"I deserve at least that much."

"Yes, you do," he agreed. "As for the others, well, if you show humility maybe they'll come to trust you. The good news is this was your first mission with them, so there might not have been a whole lot of trust to begin with."

"I can only go up from here," I said.

"Exactly. Let me get you out of those," he flicked his hand and the restraints released.

"Thanks." *Must be motion activated. Or he used his magic,* I thought. Not that I'd felt anything, but I knew that some forms of magic could be discrete. It wasn't all fireballs and lightning.

"Your armor is back in your room. When you're ready, meet us on the..."

An alarm blared.

"Uh, captain," Frank's voice came over the intercom, "we've got company. A lot of company."

"I'm on my way," Michael said, rising and heading toward the door.

"I'm right behind you," I said, stretching my legs as I jogged behind him to the cockpit.

"They shifted out of nowhere," Frank was saying. "I think they're Crimson Marauders."

"That would be a logical assumption," Michael said, eyes fixed on the tactical display.

Dozens of icons littered the display, with the larger icons spewing forth clusters of the smaller ones. "What class are they?" I asked.

"There are half a dozen corvettes and one frigate," Reynaldo answered. "Looks like they've added hangar capacity, we've got two dozen fighters inbound."

"How soon before we're outside of the planet's gravity well?" Michael asked.

"We won't even make it out of the atmosphere at this rate," the navigator shot back. "Those fighters are coming straight for us."

"Well we're dead if we stay on the ground," Michael noted. "That much is clear. So, what are our options?"

"Abandon ship?" Frank offered.

"Actual options," Michael said in a dull done.

"We can make for the other side of the planet, maybe stay low to the ground to scramble their sensors. Then, we shoot out into space on the far side and shift."

"But if they catch on to us, they'll be there waiting," Reynaldo warned.

"They could split their forces, couldn't they?" Michael asked.

"Yeah. Box us in. Depends on how badly they want us," Frank replied. "If they want us dead, those two dozen fighters will cut us to ribbons. If they want to capture us, they'll probably wait until we're in space and then disable our engines."

Michael looked at me. "Judging by how they captured you, even after you destroyed several of their ships, they'd likely try to capture us. Make for the other side of the planet, top speed."

"Awe, I was going to use turtle speed," Frank joked. "You know, slow and steady wins the race?"

"Well today the hare is carrying rockets and lasers," Michael said. "Fly like your life depends on it."

"Hey Mags," Frank said into the intercom. "Watch the engine, I'm going to be putting her through her paces. She might blow a gasket."

"Or three," Reynaldo muttered under his breath. "Hell, the whole thing might shake apart."

"You just get us out alive, fly-boy," Maggie retorted. "Leave the old girl's ticker to me."

"Strap in everyone," Frank said. "We're in for the flight of our lives."

# Chapter 6

The *Renegade* sailed across a sea of trees as we made for the other side of the planet. The tactical display showed enemy fighters' moments away from breaching the atmosphere. Would they follow our trail or try to attack from above?

"Does this ship have any stealth capability?" I asked.

Frank laughed. "Stealth? What are we, a black ops team? No, chief, nothing."

I cast a sidelong look at Michael. He *was* Federation, had he retrofitted it with special tech?

He met my eyes and shook his head.

"Damn. Too bad."

"True stealth is almost impossible," Reynaldo chimed in. "A ship either gives off heat, radiation, or noise of some kind. It's easier to hide near a source of heat, like a star or gas giant, but that poses its risks to the ship hiding. One discharge of your weapon deep in the atmosphere of a gas giant and boom," he punctuated his words with a *pow* noise and by throwing his arms up in the air and then spreading them wide.

"I get the picture," I said. *It was just an idea,* I added to myself.

"Almost there," Frank said, a few tense minutes later. "Beginning my ascent."

The view out the forward viewport changed from trees as far as the eye could see on the horizon to a blue sky. The afterburners kicked in and for a brief moment I was pressed against my seat before the inertial dampeners kicked in. Blue sky gave way to darkness a few tense moments later and the artificial gravity engaged.

"Okay, enemy ships are in hot pursuit," Reynaldo announced, interpreting the tactical display. "They're rising, but they're only about halfway around the planet."

"We've got bigger problems," Frank said, pointing. "Three corvettes blocking our path."

"Shit," Michael said.

"Send me out there," I said, moving to unstrap myself. "I'll destroy them."

"No, it's too risky. You're dangerous, but in the time you destroy one or two of those things the rest will be on top of us and have destroyed or captured us."

I kicked myself, realizing he was right.

"And besides, you promised to work as a team, remember?"

"Yes, sir," I said. *Way to go, Rachel, first combat situation after your meltdown and you want to go solo again.*

"You have the right idea, though. We need to do something unexpected. Frank, head for that central corvette's docking bay."

"Sir?" Frank asked, turning around in his seat, eyes wide. "You just talked about her plan," he pointed at me, "being suicidal for us, and now you want to bring us into the belly of the beast?"

"Their fighters are all deployed," Michael began, "and that means their docking bay will be open but not occupied. We fly in, close the outer blast doors, then commandeer the ship and shift out before the others can react."

"That's going to require a lot of speed," I said.

"And assumes they want us alive," Reynaldo said. "They could just blow up the captured corvette with us on it."

"Or override the blast doors and destroy the *Renegade*," Frank said.

"They want us alive, or they'd have bombarded us from orbit," Michael said. "No, they're going to too much trouble to capture us. Let's use that against them."

"We're running out of time," I pointed out. "Every minute we delay the enemy fighters get closer."

"Do it, Frank," Michael ordered.

Frank's eyes flicked between my face and Michael's. I kept my face smooth. Then he looked to Reynaldo.

"Just do it, man. What's the worst that can happen," the navigator said.

"We die," Frank said dryly. Then he sighed. "But I don't have a better idea, so here we go." He swiveled around and angled us toward the center corvette, then hit the afterburners again and sped toward our target at top speed."

"Grab what gear you can," Michael ordered. He flipped on the intercom. "Maggie, sorry to keep you in the dark, but things are happening fast up here. We're heading into the hangar bay of a corvette. When we land, I need you to close the hangar doors and disable them. Can you do that?"

"Sure thing, boss," she said. She offered no arguments, for which I was thankful. There was a time for arguing, and Maggie understood this wasn't the time.

"Rachel, run interference on the first wave of attackers to come through the door from further in the ship. Use your gravity well to deflect their shots while the three of us get some weapons and get into position. Then we move as a *team* further into the ship, eliminate hostiles, and make for the bridge. We secure the bridge, preferably before they can activate the self-destruct or call for help, and Frank shifts us out. Am I clear?"

"Clear," I said.

"Clear as mud," Reynaldo said.

"Here we come," Frank announced. "Landing in twenty seconds."

I leaped out of my seat and raced for the ramp. There was no time to don any armor or grab weapons, but I reached for the flickering darkness floating in a corner of my brain and readied my powers in front of the raised ramp. *Here goes everything,* I thought.

Maggie ran up from the engine room and made for her quarters to grab her gear, while footfalls from behind heralded Michael and Reynaldo doing the same.

A thud ran through my feet.

"We're docked," Frank confirmed a second later. "Lowering the ramp."

I took a breath I didn't need and sprinted down the ramp. In front of me, the blackness of space met the force field holding the air inside the docking bay. No weapon fire met me, but I drew upon my power and formed it into a vertical spinning shield as I stepped to the left and from behind the *Renegade.*

*Fwoop,* a bright red laser bolt burned into the floor a few feet to my right. Another flew over my head. A third impacted the event horizon of my shield, for I felt my energy growing and the shield increasing infinitesimally. It took much more than a small arms laser bolt to fill up my gravity well, but enough energy would make it grow larger and larger unless I took firm control and funneled some of the energy away to purposely shrink it.

*That's it, focus on me, boys,* I thought, assuming most of the pirate crew would be male. I activated my commlink. "I got their attention. Ready for you, Maggie."

"Moving," Maggie said shortly, then I heard the clang of boots and saw the engineer racing toward a corner of the hangar out of the corner of my eye. Heavy metal boxes concealed her from the enemy fire after a few seconds of running.

"On your six," Michael said, before he, Frank and Reynaldo came out in their combat armor and spread out in the area to my right. Frank and Reynaldo knelt behind two crates, while Michael knelt in the open and fired.

*Is he crazy?* I thought.

A laser flashed in front of him and I jumped. Had he been hit? I opened my mouth to shout "man down," but stopped as I saw him continuing to return fire and no sign of damage to his armor.

"Magic," he called through the speaker of his helmet. "Shield of air."

"Oh, right," I said. I'd half-forgotten he was a mage. Combat mages could turn the tide of ground battles if left unchecked, which was the reason both sides of any conflict prized mages. The mages would cancel each other out in a perfect world, while the grunts duked it out.

"Press forward," Michael ordered.

"On it," I said. I didn't have my helmet, so he was likely communicating with the team via commlink and with me through his helmet speaker. It explained the closer proximity to me, too.

A metallic screech behind me heralded the closing of the blast doors.

I moved forward, a spinning disk of gravity preceding me. Laser fire from my comrades continued, with Maggie joining us.

I stepped over the bodies of fallen pirates as we reached the door leading into the ship. I shrank my singularity to the size of my torso only so that I could see over it.

"Maggie, do you know the layout of a ship of this class?" Michael asked.

"That would have been good to ask *before* we decided to invade it," Reynaldo quipped.

"Take a left inside and then a right and another left at the fork," Maggie said. "These corvettes are all the same, with the bridge up front."

"See?" Michael said. "Give your engineer more credit, Reynaldo."

"His doubt fuels me to learn all I can," Maggie said.

"Let's move," Michael said. "Reina, you go left, I'll shield our right continue watching our six. Move fast but don't leave the team behind. Oh, and here," he tossed me a laser pistol. "When we get to the bridge, set for stun. I'd like to capture at least one of these scums this time."

I holstered the pistol in my belt in case I needed it. "Got it," I said. I leaped through the door, wearing no armor, and widened my singularity to encircle me on my right and left.

Lasers from both directions met me, so I waited until the others had moved through and begun returning fire before shrinking the singularity to the size of a tall shield and pressing forward down the hall to the left. *Left, right, then another left*, I repeated. Reynaldo and Frank flanked me, firing as we went and using my power as a shield for the brunt of the attacks while Maggie and Michael kept an eye on the rear, though no more attackers came from that direction.

At the fork, we went right, and a hail of lasers slammed into my singularity, forcing Frank and Reynaldo to fall in behind me as I advanced relentlessly.

"Repeater," Frank announced.

I nodded, already assuming they were using a repeating laser cannon based upon the rate of fire. "How far down the hall?"

"Other side of the next fork," Reynaldo said after poking his head around my shield.

"Okay. I'm on it." This time, I created a second singularity in front of my shield and cast it forward while shrinking my shield so I could see it. The second singularity, an orb of darkness to my eyes, though likely just a distortion of space to my enemies, floated down the hall. I nudged it with my mind, and it accelerated. When it hit the repeating cannon, it twisted it and sucked it in. The two gunners standing with it fared no better and, although three pirates behind the gunners tried to run, they couldn't outrun it and were sucked in as well. I then extinguished that orb. *Good riddance*, I thought.

"Damn," Frank said. "I would hate to have that happen to me."

"Don't get on her bad side, then," Reynaldo said.

At the now-cleared fork, I turned left while Michael continued to guard our rear. No laser fire met us this time, but the blast doors leading to the bridge were closed. "Stand ready, I'm going to tear these doors down," I said. Without preamble, I sent my shield forward and it impacted the center of the blast doors. At first, only metal groaned, but a moment later the metal of the door twisted around the singularity and began being sucked in. I let a good portion of the door collapse into it before extinguishing the singularity, leaving the twisted hulk of metal remaining to fall to the ground with a massive clang.

A flurry of scattered laser bolts flew through the gap left by the blast doors, with one hitting my shoulder and burning through my shirt.

*Activating nanite healing,* Jarvis responded, right on cue. Moments later the pain faded as the nano-swarm inside my blood moved to dull the pain and heal the burn.

Without waiting for the healing to complete, I advanced preparing a new singularity to shield us. With Maggie and Frank on my left and Michael and Reynaldo on my right, we advanced onto the bridge.

Sporadic laser fire came from half a dozen combatants hiding behind instrument panels, but their aim was poor and within moments they'd all fallen except one, who'd dropped his weapons and raised his hands in surrender.

"Reynaldo," Michael ordered as they approached their captive, "chart a course. Frank, as soon as he picks a place, punch the shadow drive. Maggie, you and Reina make your way to engineering and disable any tracking and make sure they don't have any nasty surprises waiting for us. I'll interrogate the captive and protect these two."

"Got it," I replied.

Maggie led the way out of the bridge, then to the left where I'd ripped the gunner team apart and then another right. It seemed the entire crew had come out to defeat us when we first boarded because we met no resistance until arriving in the engine room.

A blast from a shadowed corner of the engine room slammed into the wall next to me as I opened the door. "Who's there?" a man called.

"The new owners of this ship," I replied. "You can surrender, or you can fight and die. Your choice."

"Are you with the cult?"

I frowned. "The Cult of Rae? No. We're...mercenaries."

"Fine, I'll surrender," the man said after a moment of hesitation. He kicked his laser pistol out from his hiding place and then came out with his scrawny hands up, goggles on top of his brown hair. He looked barely older than me.

"Smart choice," I said, keeping my blaster trained on him but looking around. "You the only one here?"

"The other two left when the alarm sounded to see what was going on."

"Go stand by the door. Maggie, do your thing."

"Where's the tracker, twerp," Maggie demanded, ignoring me.

"Tr...tracker...what tracker?" the man said.

Maggie rolled her eyes. "Don't play games with me." She pointed her pistol at him. "Tell me the location of the tracking device this ship is equipped with or you won't survive this day."

I lifted a hand to reach out and lower the pistol in an attempt to de-escalate the situation, but a warning glance from Maggie stopped me. *She's being a little brutal, but if they track us to where we're going this will all be for naught.* Instead, I holstered my pistol and clasped my hands in front of me.

"It's interfaced into the system by the shadow drive computer. It sends out a ping when..."

"I know how they work," Maggie growled. "Watch him," she snapped at me before making her way to the shadow drive computer.

"Hey, girls," Frank's voice came over the ship-wide intercom, "we've got a destination...finally, and are preparing to shift. Everything good back there?"

I went to the nearest intercom speaker and activated it. "Yeah, we've secured the engine room and have another captive. Maggie is disabling the tracker, but we can shift when you're ready."

"Good," Michael put in, "because the enemy fighters are almost on us and the corvettes have launched transports to breach us. Prepare to shift."

Moments later the unnamed corvette shifted to shadow space.

# Chapter 7

"I have everything under control here," Maggie said. "Go. Get this twerp to talk."

I chuckled. "All right." I pushed the engineer ahead of me and out into the hall. There were no bodies on this side of the ship - they'd all died defending the parallel hallway when we breached. "Not a lot of crew on this corvette," I noted.

The man didn't speak.

"Fine, don't talk. Let's just make sure there aren't any stowaways, shall we?" I stopped at the first door and opened it, pistol ready in one hand while my other hand kept a grip on the engineer. *No signs of life here, unless cockroaches count.* The room was filthy. I closed the door to stop the smell, then moved on to the next room. Six rooms later and I'd found no signs of living or dead pirates.

"Rooms are clear," I announced as I arrived on the bridge. "And I brought a prisoner. How long will we be in shadow space?"

"Two more hours to go," Frank said, ignoring the prisoner. "Against my better judgment."

"What's that mean?" I asked.

"Ask Reynaldo."

"Hey, I didn't hear you throwing out any better ideas," Reynaldo said. "It's the first place that came to mind!"

"What place?" I asked. *Someone tell me what the Hell is going on.*

"Reynaldo wants to go back to his old haunt," Frank began, "Gelcrist III."

"I know people there," Reynaldo said. "They can give us a place to hide and regroup until we figure out our next move."

"People," Frank mocked, "as in criminals."

"Reformed criminals," Reynaldo retorted. "They're not anymore."

"That you know of. They're more likely to stab us in the back or turn us over to the pirates than help us."

I looked at Michael and raised an eyebrow. *Please don't pull me into the middle of this.*

"We were short of options. I sided with Reynaldo because better the enemy you know, and I'm not saying they're enemies, Reynaldo, than the enemy you don't."

I shrugged and looked at Frank. "What was your choice?"

"A Federation outpost halfway across the sector," Reynaldo chimed in. "It would have taken us days to get there and then we would have had to explain why a pirate corvette was in our possession. Too many questions."

"We could have gotten a *reward* for turning it in," Frank shot back. "Money. Something we're short on right now."

"The Federation would slow us down right now," Michael said, "and besides there could be spies for the pirates within the Federation ranks. The last thing we need is them calling the pirates on us."

I resisted the urge to frown. *That's odd. He's in the Federation but doesn't want to go to a Federation outpost? What does he have to hide?*

"So instead we trust the criminal associates of Reynaldo?" Frank asked.

"It's done, Frank," Michael said, voice firm. "Now go get some rest while I interrogate our prisoners." He motioned to me. "Bring him. I'll get this one." He bent down and lifted an unconscious pirate, the only one who had been on the bridge and survived. He led me to a room off the side.

"Sounds like you and your friends are disagreeing," the nervous young crewman from the engine room said as we walked.

"Shut up," I growled. *Now is not the time to air our crew's disunity with the enemy. The enemy we know.*

"He's still unconscious, so you're up first," Michael said to the younger crew member. "Put him in the chair." He pointed to a metal chair behind a desk.

I set the man in the chair, then stepped back. I'd never interrogated someone before. *Does he want me to take the lead or what?*

"Now, let's start with your name," Michael prompted.

"Ummm...I'm not telling you nothing," the younger man said. His eyes darted between Michael and me.

"You found him in the engine room?" Michael asked.

"Yes," I said.

"So not a fighter, a grease monkey," he mused, stroking his chin. "I imagine you don't want to die, am I right?"

The man didn't answer but swallowed hard and his eyes widened.

"You tell us what we want to know, and we won't space you."

"Don't tell him nothin', boy," a raspy voice said.

I started, searching for the source of the voice. *It's the other crew member.*

The older crew member from the bridge, with a grizzled face and graying hair, had sat up, hands tied behind his back. He spat. "Just wait till my associates find us."

"Well, good thing we disabled the tracker," Michael said without turning. "Now they can't find us."

"They're headed to Gelcrist III," the younger man said.

"Then that will be their grave," the older man said.

"Not that that information will do you any good," Michael said, appearing unperturbed. "You have no way of communicating it to your associates. But, if you tell us what we want to know, we will turn you over to the proper authorities on Gelcrist III. If you don't, well, you'll be floating in shadow space for the rest of your short lives."

"You don't scare us," the grizzled man said.

Michael turned and held out his hand, palm up. A flame appeared. "You should be scared. I've done my share of interrogating prisoners, and as a mage I have...unique...ways of making you talk."

"You mean torturing us," the older man said.

"It's a good thing we're not in Federation territory, isn't it? As my aunt says, sometimes the ends justify the means." The flame disappeared and he turned back to the engineer. "The information you have is very valuable to us and justifies the means. So, I'm going to start by torturing him," he gestured to the other man with a thumb over his shoulder, "in front of you so that you fully understand what is going to happen to you if you don't talk. Reina, stand him up against the wall."

I hesitated. He was right, we needed to know where the pirate base was, but did these people, even if they were pirates, deserve to be tortured, possibly to death, for the crime of being associated with the wrong side? My father would have said no, though he was a hypocrite. My cousin and aunt would have said yes, and the history books were full of them doing questionable things in the name of the greater good. *I don't want to be like either.* "What if you take him," I pointed to the prisoner on the ground, "out and torture him in the room next door. I'll stay in here and coax this guy for information." *Please agree, I don't want to ignore your instructions in front of you,* I thought, wishing he could hear my thoughts.

Michael stood still for a few seconds, searching my face, mulling over, I hoped, my proposal. After a few agonizing seconds, he nodded. "Good idea. Leave it up to the kid's imagination to fill in the blanks of what's being done." He bent down, stood the older prisoner up, and marched him toward the door. "He's all yours."

After the door slid shut, I approached the engineer. "You know, I have powers too."

"Magic?" he asked.

"Of a sort. I can control gravity."

"Wow," his eyes went wide, this time not in fear but awe. "How? I've never heard of that."

"It was an accident. I'm also undead, but you likely already knew that, right?"

"I could tell by your skin," he agreed, "and by your lack of breathing."

"Here's the thing. I've been tortured, sort of, when I was almost killed by a mob of angry people for trying to go to school as an undead. I don't wish that on anyone. You seem like a good person who maybe got caught up with the wrong crowd. Am I right?"

He nodded and frowned. "Yeah. I was recruited by a friend, or who I thought was my friend, back at university. He told me he found a ship for me to join up with and that the pay was great. My mom is sick, and I could really use the money, so joined up."

I put as much compassion into my voice as I could. *Hook, line, now sinker.* "I'm sorry to hear about your mother. I never knew mine. It sounds like you don't have any loyalty to these pirates. So, tell us what you know, and you'll get back to your mother free and clear."

He looked toward the door, perhaps pondering his freedom or his fellow pirate in the hands of Michael. At last, he looked me in the eyes. "Okay, I'll tell you what I know, but only because I didn't agree with it."

"Okay," I agreed.

"The word among the crew was that we're targeting crown princess Elaina."

"Who?" I asked.

He looked at me like I had grown a third eye. "Crown princess Elaina of the star kingdom of Zenubia. You've never heard of her?"

"I've heard of that kingdom, in passing," I said. "I'm not originally from the non-aligned planets."

"Well, it's a kingdom spanning five planets in the Zenubar system. It also has protectorates in surrounding systems. It's wealthy and they're considering joining the Federation."

"But the pirates don't want that to happen," I surmised, stroking my chin. "And so, they what, want to kill the crown princess?"

He shook his head. "No. Capture her and use her as leverage to force the queen to back out of negotiations with the Federation."

"Because the Federation being this close to the non-aligned planets officially would threaten their operations," I concluded. "Where were they going to capture her at?"

"I don't know," he said. "They just said we had men on the inside and the fleet was going to be a distraction while the inside men kidnapped her."

"Clever," I said. "So those ships that intercepted us back at Zignion V were part of the attack force? Were there other fleets?"

"We were all going to meet there and move together so we'd arrive at the designated time."

"Hmmm. Thank you for the information. I'll put in a good word with the captain and see that you're treated fairly when turned over to the authorities."

"I just want to get back to my mother," he said, hanging his head. "But if they," he nodded his head toward the door, "find out I betrayed them, they'll hunt me down."

"Let me take care of that. Stay here, I'll be back." I left the room and found Michael standing over the grizzled man's body. "What did you do?"

"He tried to grab a pistol and shoot me," he pointed to the pistol on the floor. "I eliminated him."

*I'm not sure I believe him, but there's more pressing information.* "Well good, because I was going to suggest spacing him anyways. Listen, I got information out of the engineer...." I recounted what the man had disclosed to me. "...and I still don't know where they're going, but..."

"I think they're heading to Gelcrist III," Michael cut in.

"What?" I blinked in surprise. "The same place we're going. How could you know that?"

"Something he," he pointed to the corpse of the older man, "said when the engineer told him we were going there. He said it would be our graveyard. He wouldn't have said that if he didn't know something. It's also a protectorate of the kingdom of Zenubia."

"Oh, I didn't know that," I said. *I guess my education in the Federation was a bit lacking, eh Dad?*

"See?" Reynaldo said from his navigator station. "I was right to pick this planet."

"You mean right to put us into the middle of a coming pirate attack," Frank said. "We're one ship."

"We won't be fighting the fleet," Michael said. "But I do have an idea. We rescue the crown princess."

"Why not just warn her?" Frank asked.

"Because the engineer said she has traitors in her midst," I pointed out. "If we tried to warn her, she would either not believe us or the moles inside would move the plan up."

"Right," Michael said. "We don't know who to trust in her entourage, so we'll need to get close to her and be ready to act when the attack comes. Then we foil the kidnappers while the planetary defense forces fight off the larger pirate presence. Minimal risk to the *Renegade*."

"What do we do with this corvette, though," Frank said.

"I have fake credentials we can use to land," Reynaldo chimed in.

"No. I'm not using fake credentials," Frank said.

"Would you rather be shot down or boarded?" Michael asked. "That's the only option."

"It's not the only option," I mused. "The *Renegade* is equipped with a shadow drive. Why don't we just load into the *Renegade,* stop the corvette, and float out into shadow space? Then we activate the shadow drive to exit shadow space at the end of the trip."

"I like that plan better," Frank said. "Even if it's dangerous."

"I can sync the navi-computer between the corvette and the *Renegade*," Reynaldo offered. "That way we are oriented, and it reduces the risk of going off-course."

"Do it," Michael said, cutting Frank off. "I like that idea better." He shot me a smile. "Good thinking. But up the ante and have Maggie set the self-destruct in the engine room. I don't want to leave evidence. And transfer any data we can from the corvette's computers. It might be encrypted but I'd rather have it than not."

"On it," Reynaldo said.

"Once that's done, everyone back to the *Renegade*. Fifteen minutes tops, then we're out of here. Reina, take our guest to the *Renegade* please, and stay there with him."

"Yes, sir," I said, before re-entering the room where I'd left the engineer. "Your information was very helpful, and you don't need to worry about the pirates learning about your involvement. Come on, we're heading back to our ship." I stepped up to him and unbound him from the chair.

His eyes widened as he stood and rubbed his arms. "I'm safe?"

"Yep," I said. "Follow me."

A few minutes later, I'd stowed the engineer, whose name turned out to be Gustav, in the "prison" quarters aboard the *Renegade* and waited for the others on the bridge. *The calm before the storm*, I thought. *What kind of fight are we walking into?*

# Chapter 8

A little over two hours later the *Renegade* emerged from shadow space. I looked out at Gelcrist III, a temperate-looking planet with green continents, blue oceans, and clouds. *Like most every planet in the Federation.* Only we weren't in the Federation.

"There's a reason Zenubia chose to make this system a protectorate of theirs," Michael said as if reading my mind. "Planets with these ecosystems are rare in this region of space, so it made sense that they would want to 'protect' a planet like this. Most planets are deserts or volcanic planets."

"I do remember that from my education," I said. There was a reason the Federation hadn't stretched in this direction, aside from the threat of the Empire striking if they stretched too thin. It wasn't economically viable to colonize uninhabitable planets.

"Looks like the party hasn't started yet," Reynaldo said.

"Lucky us," Frank said, deadpan.

The comm crackled to life. "Starship *Renegade*, this is the H.M.S. *Radiance.* You are entering royal space. Please transmit your crew and cargo manifest at once."

Frank groaned before opening his end of the channel. "Acknowledged, *Radiance.* Standby for transmission." He started tapping on his console.

I studied the *Radiance* as we neared it. It looked analogous to a Federation heavy destroyer or light cruiser in size, but the similarities ended there. It looked like a saucer with twin engines sprouting from the back. Thrusters on the port and starboard side fired to keep it in a stationary position as I watched.

"Transmission complete," Frank replied at last, before muting the comm.

"Please hold your position," the operator from the *Radiance* replied.

"Security is tighter than I remember," Reynaldo said.

"Further evidence that the princess is here," Michael said. "I recognize that ship," he pointed to another, larger, vessel, "from previous encounters. The H.M.S. *Exalted*."

"What exalted and radiant names," Frank said.

"They're all like that," Reynaldo said. "They like to talk about how 'holy' and 'sanctified' they are. I guess naming their ships is a way to cover up how they treat some of their citizens."

I rolled my eyes at that. *My father would fit in well in this kingdom.* "And there are criminals here?" I asked.

"The brightest light casts the darkest shadows," Michael said.

"Isn't that the truth," I said, thinking of my father.

"*Renegade*, this is the *Radiance*. You are clear to proceed. Traffic control will you direct you to a landing pad as you near the planet."

Frank unmuted his comm. "Acknowledged, *Radiance*, thank you." He clicked it off. "That wasn't so hard."

"Did you think they'd stop us?" I asked.

"Or did you hope they would?" Reynaldo asked.

Frank shot Reynaldo a sharp look. "No. I just thought with security this high they'd ask us some questions or something."

"Like 'do you agree that the queen of Zenubia is the holiest of holy'?" Reynaldo quipped.

"Or 'on a scale of one to ten, how holy are you'?" I joked.

"Shut up, the lot of you," Frank said, though the humor in his voice betrayed his words.

"All right let's look alive," Michael said. "Depending on where they have us land, we might have to procure ground transportation to get to the princess' location."

"Don't we have to find where she's at first?" Reynaldo asked.

"Start scanning the frequencies for any chatter about the princess being here. Even encrypted channels might betray the source and give us a clue."

"On it," Reynaldo said.

"How long before the Crimson Marauders attack, do you think?" I asked.

"I honestly expected them to be here by now," Michael said. "It worries me."

"Why?"

He looked me in the eyes. "Because they could be taking the time to prepare an even larger assault force than we expect. Which could be bad for us."

"True," I acknowledged, "but you said yourself they want her alive. They'll still need to come down and get her, no matter how many ships they bring."

"Yes, but if they control the orbital space then we'll have a hell of a time getting her off the planet," Michael pointed out. "I'm counting on the Zenubian fleet defeating the Crimson Marauders if we hold off their snatch-and-grab team long enough. But if they're overwhelmed..." he trailed off.

"...then it makes our job a whole lot harder," I admitted.

"Nothing we can't handle," Frank said. "What with you two on the case, they'll be quaking in their boots. Just send the rogue girl wonder up to crush their fleets."

My cheeks would have warmed with embarrassment if I'd been alive. Would I ever live down going rogue? How long before the team trusted me to stick around in the heat of battle? I held my tongue.

The next few minutes passed in awkward silence from the four of us as Reynaldo sifted through various communication channels in the background.

The comm crackled to life. "Starship *Renegade*, this is Gelcrist III traffic control. Please state your destination and business."

"What's our business?" Frank asked.

"Tell them we're spice merchants, and our destination is...one second," Reynaldo studied a map that had appeared on his holo-display, "Valamere City."

"Is that near where the princess is?" Michael asked.

"I think so. An awful lot of law enforcement and encrypted chatter in that area."

Frank opened his end of the comm. "Gelcrist III traffic control, this is the *Renegade*. We are spice traders destined for Valamere City. Transmitting credentials now."

"Acknowledged *Renegade*. You may proceed, but you will be subject to a customs exam upon landing."

"Understood, control," Frank said before closing the link. "Well shit."

"Didn't we expect this?" I asked. "Wouldn't customs want to check our credentials regardless of the planet?"

"Credentials, sure," Frank said. "I transmitted those. But an *exam*, they only do those when they're suspicious of something."

"Likely due to the heightened security," Michael said.

"That doesn't mean they won't know we aren't merchants the second they see the inside of our ship," Frank snapped.

"So, we'll say we're empty, awaiting cargo," Michael fired back.

"We don't have a cargo hold," Frank said through clenched teeth.

Michael sighed. "Point taken."

"I...may have a way to get the customs exam waived," Reynaldo said.

Frank glared at him. "No."

"Your associates?" I surmised.

"Former associates," Reynaldo said. "But yeah, they have...connections in customs. I can make a call and get us through."

"Do it," Michael said, shooting a warning glance at Frank. "We don't have other options right now. I don't like circumventing the law either, but sometimes the ends justify the means."

*Sounds like my aunt Bridgette*, I thought sourly.

Reynaldo turned to his station, preparing to make the call.

"I'm going to check on Gustav. I mean the prisoner" I said, standing up. *Don't get too familiar with him,* I chastised myself. I made my way to the makeshift prison cell and stepped inside.

Gustav sat on his bunk, staring at the wall. He looked up when I entered. "I take it we're at Gelcrist III?"

"We are," I said. "We're going to be landing soon, then working to save the princess. You're going to stay here while we do that. Frank will be watching the ship."

"I could be useful, you know," he said. "I know a little about the pirates, and I could help fight?"

"Do you even know your way around a pistol?" I asked.

"Not...not really," he admitted.

"I didn't think so. Thank you for the offer, but we can't afford to trust you, the mission is too important."

"So what, I'm just going to rot in here forever?"

"No. After we rescue the princess, we'll turn you over to the proper authorities, just like I said before. They can take it from there."

"Great. So I can rot in a Zenubian prison for the rest of my life. They don't take a lenient view on crime, you know."

"So I've heard." *All honor and nobleness and bullshit,* I thought. "I know you want to get back to your mother, but actions have consequences."

"I just wish I could redeem myself," he said, hanging his head.

"Can I get you anything?" I asked, ignoring his statement. *Now is not the time for pity.*

"Just some water and something to eat," he asked. "If that's not too much to ask."

"I'll be back," I said, closing the door and heading to the kitchen area. As I poured water into a glass and grabbed a pair of ration bars, the best we could do under the circumstances, my thoughts drifted to my past. Why did I feel pity for the engineer, despite knowing he was aligned with an evil pirate group? If he'd fired a shot at me back on the corvette, I'd have killed him on the spot, never knowing his story. But everyone had a story, so why did his stick in my mind? *Maybe because he has a mother to go home to.* I'd never known my mother, what with her being killed by the Empire shortly after I was born. My father had gone to war, at least in part, to avenge her death, but that didn't ease my pain. *She was taken from me by bad people, just like Gustav was essentially taken from his mother by bad people.*

*Knock it off,* I chastised myself. *Focus on the mission.* I carried the water and ration bars back to Gustav's cell and opened the door. "Here," I said, offering the items. "It's the best I can do right now. Sit tight, we should be in and out."

"Good luck out there," Gustav said. "Don't underestimate the Crimson Marauders. They're not all mindless buffoons."

"And I'm no ordinary soldier," I countered, annoyed. "We'll see who surprises who." I closed the door and headed back toward the cockpit.

"Are we close?" I asked as I entered the cockpit.

"Almost there," Frank said.

"Three minutes out," Michael expanded.

"Did you contact your associates, Reynaldo?"

"Yeah," he said sounding subdued. "I made the arrangements. Someone will meet us at the docking bay."

"Ask him about the terms," Frank said.

*Of course there'd be terms.* "Reynaldo?"

"They want money...," he began.

"And...," Frank prompted.

"Weapons," Reynaldo finished.

"Oh," I said. I looked at Michael. "Are we going to give it to them?"

"I'm hoping they'll accept, and I owe you, but we don't have a choice, do we? If customs inspect us, they'll see right through the subterfuge and we risk fighting Zenubian's citizens."

"The non-corrupt ones," Reynaldo pointed out. "Some of the princess's retinue are corrupt."

"Correct. I want to avoid bloodshed if possible," Michael said.

I sighed. "It sounds shady, but you're right, we don't have a choice."

"I'm going to pay them the money up-front, then promise the weapons later."

"Do you think they'll go for it?"

"It's that or we offer them the weapons we have aboard the *Renegade*, but I don't think they'll want those."

"One minute out," Frank announced.

"Let's gear up," Michael ordered. "Frank, you stay here to guard the ship and the prisoner."

"And to keep his associates from robbing the place while you're gone," Frank said, shooting Reynaldo a glare again before turning his attention to landing, flicking switches, and turning knobs.

"Just keep the engines warm," Michael said, ignoring the jab. "The four of us are going to find the princess."

The three of us from the cockpit left and geared up, then met Maggie in the common area near the ramp controls. "Ready?" she asked. "I heard about the arrangement," she said when Reynaldo opened his mouth.

I nodded inside my armor, with the helmet retracted, and Michael and Reynaldo followed suit.

"Let's greet the welcome wagon."

The ramp descended and we were met with the sight of about a dozen figures in tunics and trousers wearing bandoleers laden with grenades across their bodies and with rifles in hands. Fortunately, the rifles were pointed at the ground.

The lead man watched them descend the ramp, eyes locked on Reynaldo. Then he smiled wide and spread his arms. "Reynaldo, you old scoundrel!"

"Hey, Chuck," Reynaldo said, sounding like he was forcing the enthusiasm into his voice. "Long time, no see."

Chuck approached and hugged Reynaldo, then stepped back and appraised the three of us. "These your new friends?" he asked.

"More like co-workers," Reynaldo said. "I'm a mercenary now."

Chuck pursed his lips. "A mercenary, you say? Good for you, Rey."

"Rey?" I blurted out, surprised.

"He didn't tell you? That was his nickname, back in the day."

*Wait till Frank hears about* that.

"That was a long time ago," Reynaldo said.

"The family still misses you," Chuck said. "Ol' Gran kicked the bucket and where was Rey? Nowhere to be found."

"You're related?" Michael and I asked in unison, sharing shocked expressions.

Chuck put a hand over his chest. "I'm wounded. Of course we're related. He's my cousin!"

"Exploiting your cousin," Michael said. "Not very family-like."

Chuck shrugged. "It's just business. Times are tough around these parts."

"Are you gangsters?" I asked.

"Mafia, technically," Chuck said, smiling. "At your pleasure."

I resisted the urge to roll my eyes.

"Here are the credits," Michael said, handing over a credit chip. "We'll get you the weapons later. We don't have anything you'd be interested in right now. But there's going to be a lot of fighting soon, so you can probably scavenge some weapons in the chaos following the fight?"

"Fighting?" Chuck asked. "Rey didn't say nothing about no fighting. Who you plan on fighting?"

"The Crimson Marauders are on their way here," Michael said. "We're going to stop them from kidnapping a high-value target."

"That band of pirate blowhards is heading *here*?" Chuck said. "With what navy?"

"They've been building up," Reynaldo said. "And they're just here for the princess."

I shot him a glance. *Way to tip our hand as to who the high-value target is.*

Chuck whistled. "Princess Elaina, eh? I heard she was in town. So, you're gonna swoop in and what, save her?"

"That's the plan," Michael said.

"I hope you ain't expecting help from us," Chuck said. "We ain't the battlin' type."

"That's obvious," Maggie said, speaking for the first time since we'd come out of the ship.

"Don't worry, this is our fight, not yours," Michael reassured him. "As I said, there'll be weapons lying around after the battle. I'm hoping you'll count those as our payment."

Chuck pursed his lips for a long moment. "Yeah, that'll work." He grinned. "The least I can do for my little cousin."

"We need to go," Michael said, "before the..."

A series of sonic booms, followed by air raid sirens, interrupted him.

"...assault begins."

# Chapter 9

"We need to find the princess, now," Michael said. He looked at Chuck and raised an eyebrow.

"We came here in a few speeders. I suppose we could let you borrow one."

"And the princess? Do you know where she was supposed to be?"

"Let me make a few calls," he said. He pulled out his communicator. "Oi, Billy, it's Chuck. Where's that princess supposed to be today. Yeah, Elaina, where was she today? You don't know? You don't know? Well, find somebody who does, Billy. Yeah, I'll wait." He looked up. "He's gettin' it."

Michael looked to Reynaldo. "Any ideas?"

The navigator shook his head. "I pinpointed it to his city, but I don't know specifically where they are inside the city," he said.

"I could fly up," I whispered. "See what I can see."

"No, it's too much risk of someone seeing you," Michael said. "Not to mention these clowns," he gestured discreetly to the mafia members in front of them.

"All right, thanks Billy," Chuck said, turning off the communicator. "Bill says they're over at the Holy See for some peace ceremony."

I made a gagging motion. The hypocrisy of the Zenubian kingdom sickened me.

"Okay. Where is that?" Michael said, sounding impatient.

"Just put 'Holy See' into the navigator of your speeder," Chuck said. "Here's the keys to the one at the very end of the line out front." He tossed Michael a key dongle.

"Thank you," Michael said. "Let's move."

We wasted no time leaving the docking bay housing the *Renegade* and locating the speeder Chuck had identified. No customs officials stopped us. There weren't even any officials around. *Thanks to the mafia, no doubt*, I thought. If there had been, they'd likely have been alarmed by armed and armored figures leaving a docking bay without being inspected first.

We piled into the speeder, with Michael driving, Reynaldo riding shotgun, and Maggie and me in the back. Reynaldo punched in the coordinates. "Five minutes away," he said.

"Not if I have anything to say about it," Michael said. He left the line of speeders and accelerated hard, pressing us back in our seats. We flashed past modern-looking buildings and throngs of people looking up and pointing at the sky. It was a landspeeder, so It couldn't fly, but traffic was light and didn't impede our progress.

As we neared the destination, with the navigation control predicting one minute to our destination, Michael slowed. "Police cordon ahead," he warned. Indeed, a line of police vehicles blocked the road. Behind them rose a tall building of what looked like a stone of some kind. *Must be the Holy See*, I thought. Above, dropships continued to stream into the atmosphere, and what looked like a pair of fighters flew by low overhead. *How many ships did the pirates bring?* They really wanted the princess, or the kingdom, rather.

"Go down that alley," Reynaldo said, pointing.

Michael obliged and they exited the vehicle.

"How are we going to get past the police?" I asked.

"We could wait until the shooting starts?" Maggie said.

"And they start shooting at us," Michael said.

"I could fly over," I said. "I'd do it fast, and they wouldn't even notice with all the hub-bub," I said before Michael could object.

"There is a way for the rest of us," Reynaldo said, backing me up. "There is a sewer grate there," he pointed, "that should run under the street and come out by the Holy See."

Michael mulled over it. "Fine. Reina, fly over the blockade and get to the princess ASAP. That is your top priority. Understood?"

I nodded. "Yes."

"Protect her until the three of us arrive, or until her security forces reclaim the area."

"They look like they have it under control already," I pointed out.

"Those drop pods say otherwise," Michael said. "They're likely landing blocks away and moving in with a coordinated strike." He paused, tilting his head to one side. "Oh."

"What?" I asked.

"Magic," he said. "They have mages with them."

"That complicates things," Maggie said.

"Wouldn't the princess have mages in her protection detail?"

"Most likely, but some of those could be the traitors. One mage can take out a lot of mundanes."

"We'll see how they do against me," I said. "Meet you on the other side." I made sure my weapon was secured, then summoned a gravity well. I sent it high into the air above the buildings, then bound myself to it. I shot into the air and hovered, untouched by the gravity of the planet. *Oh, how I've missed this feeling*, I thought. The wind blew into me, but my gravity well held me steady.

I oriented myself toward the Holy See and sent my gravity well toward it. I followed along in its wake, like a pet owner being pulled behind a massive dog on a leash. I passed the police line in seconds and looked down to see them pointing at me. Some pointed more than fingers at me, but I ignored them, my gaze set on my destination. The Holy See had looked like a stone from afar, but as I approached, I realized it was a painted metal with glass windows set into it. *A replica. A fake, like their kingdom.*

Explosions peppered the area to the left and right of the area approached. *Must be the pirates making their move. Sorry, guys, I got here first*, she thought. Though that didn't account for the traitors in the princess's retinue. *How am I going to identify them? How am I going to identify the princess?*

I landed on top of the building and looked around. The barricades blocking four streets leading into the massive square were holding, but three were on fire. Only the barricade in the direction we'd come was still holding, and that was the direction hundreds of civilians were now flooding as panic set in.

*Now how to get in*, I thought. I jogged along the top of the Holy See looking for an emergency hatch. *There.* I went to it and using my superhuman strength pulled it off its hinges and tossed it aside. I peeked in to ensure no one was there waiting with a weapon, then jumped down. I was standing on a catwalk. A set of stairs ran along the side of the building, zigzagging to the ground floor, but today I wasn't using the stairs.

I activated my helmet and turn on the comm. "Michael, come in. I'm inside the Holy See. Where are you guys?"

At first, nothing happened, then, "I read you, Reina. We're just about to exit the sewers below the main square. Sounds like a lot of fighting above us. Might take a few minutes to reach you."

"I understand. I'll look around until you get here."

I looked over the railing. *Jarvis, amplify. I'm looking for the crown princess. Her name is Elaina. I don't know what she looks like, can you...*

*I have found a portrait of the crown princess,* Jarvis interrupted me. Thank goodness for predictive AIs. A picture displayed in my mind's eye, fed by Jarvis. The targeting system in my helmet took that image and began scanning targets. After a few seconds, the red targeting box centered on a young-looking woman on a stage wearing a white dress.

*Shit, I didn't even need the portrait. I should have known look for the holiest-dressed woman in the place.* Wearing white to proclaim her piety and morality. *She'll be real fun in conversation. Not.*

Several guards surrounded the dais, wearing ceremonial cloth uniforms and old-fashioned metal helmets. *Not very protective.* Their weapons weren't old-fashioned, however, with them carrying submachine guns in their hands and pistols on their sides. Other guards stood in front of the pillars that lined the building, though whether they were necessary for holding up the building or just for show was anyone's guess.

The guests, like those outside the building, were evacuated through the main doors, ushered by guards. Several guests wore dresses or suits. It had been a formal event of some sort.

I could easily float down to the princess, but I knew if I did that her guards were more apt to shoot first and ask questions later. *Should I call up to her from up here? Tell her I come in peace? No, she probably wouldn't believe it, and they'd start shooting anyway.* Or, even worse, the traitors would show their colors and start shooting the good guards or make a getaway with the princess.

A thump on the roof above me interrupted my thoughts. *Sounds like a transport,* I thought. I moved away from the direct line of sight below the hatch and crouched, waiting.

Moments later, a pair of figures in crimson armor climbed down the stairs, their backs to me.

I moved before the first figure could put more than a foot on the catwalk. Charging forward I slammed his head against a rung of the ladder, then, with them dazed enough to let go of the rungs, I threw him off the catwalk.

The second figure scrambled for his rifle one-handed, but I didn't give him the chance. I yanked his leg and, using my strength combined with his one-handed grip on the ladder, whipped him off the ladder and also tossed him off the catwalk. I looked over the edge and found their crumpled bodies lying on the floor and several guards looking up and pointing their weapons in my direction.

I wasted no more time on those below me, instead back up again and waiting to see if more would descend through the hatch.

A grenade soared through the hatch opening this time, but I summoned a tiny singularity and sucked the grenade into it. *Time to go,* I thought. More soldiers would be through in moments. I leaped over the edge of the catwalk, hoping that my armor not matching the crimson armor of those I'd thrown to their deaths would mark me as a friend, or at least delay their shots long enough to explain myself. I slowed my fall with a gravity well above my head so that I floated to the ground at a quarter of the gravity than normal. That performance alone seemed to cause the guards to hold their fire.

I landed in the middle of the building, a hundred feet or so from the princess. A cordon of guards had formed between me and her. *Don't want to be too close.* I bowed. "Crown Princess Elaina, your life is in danger."

"I am not a half-whit, stranger, I can see the enemy approaching," the crown princess's voice floated up from behind her guards. She sounded about my age. "But I am quite safe here. You, on the other hand, are a moment away from death. Identify yourself."

*Rachel Darklance, daughter of the supreme commander of the Federation*, I thought, but knew I couldn't say that. "My name is Reina, and I'm an ally with critical information."

"I'm listening," the crown princess said. "First tell me who those men were you threw to their deaths."

"They're with the Crimson Marauders," I said. "They are here to kidnap you."

The princess laughed, a lilting, dainty sound. "They will surely fail. That is not a credible threat."

"There's more," I said. I hesitated, then summoned singularities behind me and on my flanks, then continued. "I have it on credible authority that there are traitors among your guard retinue. They are working hand-in-hand with the Crimson Marauders to capture you."

"Preposterous," the princess said, though I sensed hesitation creeping into her voice. "My guards would not betray me."

"Enough of this!" one of her guards, this one near the center of the formation in front of me, shouted. "Guards, fire!"

"Wait!" the princess said, but too late. Several guards opened fire with their automatic weapons.

I expanded the singularities around me and summoned one in front of me also. The bullets disappeared into the gravity wells, but that didn't stop them from continuing to fire. I looked up and saw a dozen or more crimson-armored individuals leaning over the railing. *It's a distraction.*

"Stop!" the princess roared and slowly the fire died down. "Captain Maynard, why did you order your guards to shoot?"

"Because she is a liar, your highness," he said gruffly.

"I am not so sure," the princess said.

The guard, Captain Maynard, looked up, then shook his head. "It doesn't matter now. Marauders, attack!" He suited the action to words and turned his rifle and fired on several of the guards in the building. Several guards near him followed suit. Their prey fell, stunned, before the onslaught.

*Well, there's the traitor*, I thought. I rose into the air to gain a vantage point to see the princess.

She stood in the center of what had been a friendly echelon but now the bodies of several guards lay littered around her and two traitorous guards had her pinned on the ground and were putting her in shackles. "Traitors!" she shouted. "Unhand me at once!"

A commotion near the main entrance caught my eye. Several guards entered, though they had yet to open fire on the traitors.

*More traitors?* I wondered.

Captain Maynard looked up. "You want to take them?" he called up.

A man and a woman not wearing armor but wearing robes leaped off the catwalk and instead of falling, they fell like leaves on the wind. They landed between me and the main entrance.

My eyes narrowed. Did they have my powers or...no, I felt the wind rushing past me. They were using air magic to slow their fall.

"With pleasure," the female mage said. She summoned a fireball and launched it toward the newcomer guards. It exploded in their midst before most could do more than jump aside and set several of them on fire. When the survivors returned fire, the bullets slammed into an invisible barrier. Lightning crackled between the woman's fingers and she stretched out her arm, unleashing a torrent of lightning that connected with the survivors instantly and electrocuted them. At last, she turned and looked up at me. "So, you're the gnat making trouble for my organization."

I floated where I was, thinking of a plan. *Keep her talking.* "You know it. Who are you?"

"Oh, you don't need to know my name," she said. "I'll be the last sight you ever see, deary."

"I wouldn't count me out yet," I said, summoning gravity wells. I hesitated, debating between heading toward the princess to protect her or going on the offensive and striking at these mages. *They could run out the back with the princess if I don't protect her*, I thought. That settled it. I sent my gravity well toward the space above the princess and prepared to sail along behind it.

A jolt of pain shuddered through my body at that moment.

*Warning, electrical discharge detected*, Jarvis alerted me.

*No...shit,* I said through clenched teeth as I fought against unconsciousness and fought to stay floating. I extinguished the gravity well I was meant to follow and instead turned back to the enemy mage. Maybe it had been a mistake to turn my back on her.

"Resilient," the woman said. "Let's see how you handle fire." She summoned a fireball this time and sent it soaring toward me.

I summoned a gravity well and placed it between us. It absorbed the fire when it was halfway to me.

"Clever girl. Some sort of gravity magic. I almost didn't believe the reports when I first heard of you." She smiled a wicked smile. "Let's see how many directions you can defend against."

This time she and the male mage each used magic, with fire spreading from the woman and snaking toward me from multiple directions and ice shards coming at me from at least two directions.

I created a cocoon of gravity this time, creating equal and opposite gravity wells to both protect me and keep me steady in one location. I expanded each into a narrow disk of a singularity for maximum coverage. *Their attacks won't get through.*

At the last second, however, another shock of lightning, this time stronger than before, slipped around the shield between me and the female mage. It caused every muscle in my body to tense up and my shields faltered as I screamed, and Jarvis screeched warnings. Then the flames and ice slammed into my body, the fire scorching every nerve on the outside of my body and roasting my insides, while the ice impaled me. This time Jarvis warned of imminent death and I screamed louder than I ever had. *This is it; this is when I die for good.* There was nothing I could do.

I tried to draw on the last of my power, perhaps to form a final singularity to escape into, ending my suffering early. In that moment of extreme agony, I felt something "open" inside of me. That's the only word I can use to describe it. Like a door opening to let in a cool breeze, something opened up in my mind, and then suddenly the pain subsided. I opened my eyes and saw colored lines stretching from the mages to the fire and ice and lightning. I breathed in, for the first time since I died feeling a need to do so, and the lines grew thicker. Feeling like I had in the gravity generator back during basic training, I "drew in" the power, like sucking in breath, and it flooded into my body, but this time it did not burn or freeze me. It filled me like a thousand water hoses filling a reservoir at once. I felt full and fulfilled at once, like I could both explode and shout with glee.

*Energy levels critical*, Jarvis warned.

*What do I do?* I asked him. I didn't *want* the flow of power to end. I wanted it to fill me forever.

*Unknown.*

I looked toward the unnamed man and woman and saw what looked like fear in their eyes. She looked older somehow, too.

*I'll unleash it*, I thought. I closed my eyes and reached for that reservoir of raw power, raw magic, I realized, and lifted my arms. I envisioned the energy channeling through my arms and coalescing before my palms. It did. I smiled, pushing more energy into the channels. The dual orbs of raw energy grew ever larger, looking reddish-purple to my eyes. Then I aimed as best I could and "exhaled." The energy surged like dual beams of death toward the enemy mages, whose screams of pain or fear were cut off as their bodies were disintegrated before the force of my power.

With the remaining power I had left, I turned and splayed my fingers wide. The beams split into ten smaller beams, like trickles, but those trickles burned holes in the princess's captors as she lay in the center of the maelstrom, unharmed.

*I did it*, I thought. *I saved the princess.*

*Power levels low. Shut down imminent,* Jarvis warned. *Initiating nano-swarm.*

I fell and darkness took me before I hit the ground.

# Chapter 10

I woke to silence. And pain. Not the pain of being attacked from before, but the pain of a healing body. I sat up, slowly, and looked around. I was in my quarters, with an IV sticking out my arm.

*Healing at ninety-five percent*, Jarvis reported.

"Ah, good, you're awake," Michael said. He sat at my bedside.

My lips were dry. I cleared my throat before sitting up and trying to speak. "What...what happened?"

"What's the last thing you remember?" he countered.

"I was fighting two mages and," I coughed, then continued, "something happened. I saved the princess." I did remember that much.

Michael nodded. "We arrived moments after I felt a colossal surge of power, then nothing. That power, it was stronger than even my...," he cut off, "...instructor at school by far."

I cringed. "That was me." I relayed the story of the fight. "So, then I killed the two mages and the traitorous guards who had captured the princess. Then I passed out."

"*You* were the source of that surge? How? You don't have magic."

I shrugged, then cringed from a twinge of sharp pain. "I don't know for sure. It was like I sucked in their magic and I could suddenly see these ropes or..."

"Flows," he said quietly.

"Yes. Like flows. And I sucked them in and felt like I was being supercharged or something and then I just unleashed it in this raw torrent."

"I see." He sat solemn and silent for a long moment. "Close your eyes."

"Okay," I said, closing my eyes. "Now what?"

"Hold out your hand. Now imagine a trickle of the power you felt before flowing down your arm and into the space above your palm. It might require you to open a door in your mind."

"I felt that door before," I said. "During the attack."

"Good. Now repeat it, but this time control the flow. Shape the raw energy into a flame. Imagine it, orange, red and white with some blue peppered in. Picture the energy forming into the flame. Morphing, if you will."

I sought the door in my mind that I'd sensed before. *Come on, there's a door for my gravity powers, or there was, there's got to be one for the elemental magic.* I found it after a long moment. The power surged through me once more and threatened to overwhelm me like it had the first time, but this time I was ready and shaped it into thin threads that flowed down my arms to my hands. There I followed

Michael's instructions and envisioned the raw energy forming into twin glowing flames. At first, nothing happened. Then I felt the heat.

"Open your eyes," Michael said.

I opened my eyes and focused on my hands. There floated two multi-colored flames, warming my flesh but not burning it.

"The magic will insulate you from the heat if you maintain control. There are cases where new mages," he cringed, "will burn themselves by pulling in too much heat and burning themselves, or vice-versa and freezing their flesh, but if you control your magic and maintain a balance you should be fine."

"Sounds a bit dangerous," I joked. "I don't think I can destroy myself in a singularity." *Though I was about to try back in the Holy See.*

"There are more elements to control," he replied. "Instead of a single physical element, gravity, you are trying to juggle fire, water in all its forms, lightning, air or wind and earth and its derivatives. Some mages can even control light. Not all mages are specialized in all magics. Some are strongest in two while weaker in the rest. Others are 'normal,' for lack of a better term, across all elements, with no one element being stronger than the rest objectively."

"So how do I know which element I'm strongest in?"

"It will take time and experimentation. There are measurement tools we can use, but I don't have any of them here. But judging by the recounting of your performance and the raw power I felt, you could be a strong mage all-around."

"What if I don't want to be a mage?" I asked.

Michael smiled. "We don't get to choose to be mages. If there's a god, perhaps he or she chooses for us to be mages, but I'm not sure I believe that."

"He'd be a pretty shitty god," I agreed. "To allow so much suffering in this world. So, I'm stuck being a mage, fine. When do I start training?"

"Not yet, I'm afraid. There's a...situation we have to deal with first."

"What kind of situation?" I asked

"You can come in," Michael called toward the door.

The door slid open and a blond woman about my age stood there in a too-large jumpsuit. Her face was marred by scrapes and she wore a scowl. "You rang?" she asked, voice dripping with sarcasm.

"Reina, this is the crown princess of Zenubia, Princess Elaina."

I lifted a hand in greeting. "Hello."

The princess sniffed. "I suppose I should thank you for saving me from being kidnapped. Except for your *associate*, she directed a glare at Michael, seems to have kidnapped me, so I'm no better off."

Michael sighed. "As I told you, Your Highness, we don't know who to trust among your guard retinue. You're safer here than among your security forces until the fighting dies down."

"And I'm telling you that there are agents I can trust here," the princess aid. "If you'd just let me leave this bucket of bolts to go get them."

"You're holding her prisoner?" I asked, incredulous.

"Not exactly," Michael said, blushing. "She's in protective custody."

I snorted. "I wouldn't like being a prisoner, I mean, in protective custody, either. Not many would." *And this princess is not one to sit idly by and accept her fate, that's for sure.*

"See? Even your crew side against you," Elana said.

"She's new," Michael said as a way of explanation. He cleared his throat. "The fact remains the fighting is ongoing and it's not safe here for you."

The princess snorted. "As if the Crimson Marauders stand a chance against the royal navy. I'm certain reinforcements are on their way as we speak."

"And I'm sure the pirates are aware of that and are going to shift out-system soon," Michael acknowledged. "Until then, we need to lay low. Once they're gone, you can identify who you think you can trust, and we'll hand you off to them."

"But that doesn't get us any closer to stopping them for good," I said.

"What do you mean?" the princess asked, frowning.

"We're trying to locate the main pirate base of operation," I said. "If they get away, we'll never find it."

"So, what do you suggest? Following the pirates?"

"I know that look," Michael said. "What are you thinking?"

"I thought she was new," the princess asked. "Yet you know her 'look' already?"

"I've been around a long time," Michael said. "I'm good at reading people. *And* dealing with royalty," he cast a meaningful glance toward the princess.

*Says the guy who looks barely older than me,* I thought. Maybe he used nanite skin treatments to look younger. "What if we claim we have the princess as our captive..."

"Which you do, technically," the princess chimed in.

"...and use that as a way to find the pirate base?"

"It's risky," Michael said.

"And foolish," Elaina added. "I'm not staying on this ship a moment longer than necessary.

"Uh, captain," Frank's voice came over the comm. "We've got a situation."

Michael rose and activated the intercom. "What is it?"

"I had Maggie hack into the nearby security cameras. We've got some shady-looking characters heading our way."

"Are they Reynaldo's friends, err, family?" I asked.

"Don't look like it. His cousin and crew jetted shortly after you. These guys are in Zenubian uniforms, but they don't look very...regal."

I rolled my eyes. "You think they're impostors?"

"That would be my guess," Frank replied. "They're searching every berth and are heavily armed."

"Okay, raise the ramp and prepare to lift off. I'm on my way to the cockpit."

"Copy that," Frank said. The link closed.

"Shouldn't we at least wait for them to arrive so I can see if I know them?" Elaina asked. "For all you know they could be my official guards."

"The same 'official guards' who were selling you out?" Michael snapped back. "No, we can't wait, we can't take the chance that they identify you and mark our ship. Our anonymity is the only thing we have going for us."

"Where will we go, then?" Elaina asked.

"We'll figure that out on the fly. The first thing is surviving."

"And there's no chance of me getting off this ship before you take off, is there?" she asked.

"Sorry, princess, that wouldn't be the responsible thing."

She shook her head and sighed, chest heaving. "Fine. I'll sit with the injured crew member."

"I have a name," I said.

She ignored my comment.

"Keep an eye on her," Michael said to me before leaving the room.

The princess stood there and I sat in silence for a few long moments. *Screw this. I'm not sitting here in silence the whole way to wherever the hell we're going.* "Did you want to sit?" I gestured to the chair Michael had just occupied."

She glared at me for a long moment, saying nothing, before sighing and taking a seat. She crossed her arms.

"I'm sorry this happened to you," I said. "I know it's not easy when your life is upended. I went through something similar when..."

"I don't want to hear your sob story," Elaina snapped. "We're not friends and I don't care."

I blinked in surprise. "Wow, I figured you were royalty, but I didn't think you'd be a royal ass to your savior."

"I told you it wasn't a rescue when I ended up in captivity again," she said.

"You're not in captivity!" I shouted.

"Then let me leave!" Elaina shouted back.

"You want to be kidnapped and used as a pawn to bring about the end of Zenubia? Fine! I'll throw you out there and you can greet these newcomers. Take your chances!"

That shut her up. For a moment, anyway. "I didn't ask for any of this," she said at last in a much more subdued tone.

*Neither did I, your royal pain in the assness*, I thought. "Few of us do," I said instead. "But we have to make do with the hand we're dealt in this life. Life isn't fair."

"No, I suppose it isn't," she agreed.

"Reina, we're about to take off," Michael said over the intercom. "Can you man the turrets? Are you feeling up to it?"

"I'm back at one hundred percent, or near enough," I began, thankful for the interruption. "I'll do it."

"Excellent. Princess, I would go strap in. There are seats in the common area."

To my surprise, the princess didn't argue. She followed me out of my quarters and obediently took her seat and strapped in.

*Once we take off it's not like she's going to go anywhere,* I thought as I made my way toward the gun seat, located halfway between the common area and the cockpit. I strapped in, donned a headset, and stared at the blank targeting screen as the ship lifted off. It flickered to life as we bee-lined for orbit, and I looked out the transparisteel canopy at the battle still ensuing above the skies of Gelcrist III. *The pirates sure put up a fight. They're probably still trying to create a distraction while some of their people search for the princess.* It was the only explanation for why the pirates would still be around.

"Look alive," Michael said through the headset as the blue of the atmosphere gave way to the darkness of space. "Oh, sorry." He cleared his throat. "I don't know if either side is going to fire on us, but chances are someone will. And Reina," he said, voice lowered, "no gravity manipulation today, am I clear?"

"Yes," I said, feel embarrassed but not defensive. "I understand." I was still on thin ice after Zignion V.

"Don't fire unless fired upon," he finished. "Self-defense only."

"You got it," I said.

The space above Gelcrist III looked like a combination of ship graveyard and battlefield. Capital ships from both sides littered the space.

*Looks like the pirates gave as good as they got,* I thought. Zenubar was not the Federation, which explained why the Crimson Marauders wanted to stop them from joining the Federation at any cost.

A pair of Zenubian fighters chased a Crimson Marauder bomber before two other Crimson Marauder fighters drove them off. Elsewhere, a Crimson Marauder frigate succumbed to a swarm of Zenubian bombers and exploded.

"We've got company," Michael announced. "Two Zenubian fighters, dead ahead."

"Shit," I said. The last thing I wanted was to shoot down Zenubian fighters. "I'll try to shoot to disable," I promised.

"We don't know if these are the traitors in disguise," Michael pointed out. "Do what you have to do."

"If you say so," I said.

We closed with the fighters fast. They flashed past us and I almost thought they were going to ignore us, but then they turned and followed us. *Shit,* I thought. Moments later, they opened fire. The shields absorbed the impact of their laser bursts.

"There's my cue," I said, targeting the first fighter. I squeezed the trigger and a stream of bullets hurtled toward what was now our foes. The first several rounds vaporized against their shields, but the tail end ripped through their hull and the first fighter exploded.

The second fighter fired again, this time with lasers and a pair of missiles, and this time the *Renegade* shook more.

"A couple more hits like that and we're space dust," Frank growled over the link. "Take them out."

"You think?" I asked, trying to put sarcasm into my voice. "Here I was eating pastries while they take potshots at us." I aimed and fired another stream of bullets. Some of them missed, but enough hit that the enemy fighter spun out and veered off. "There, got them off our tail long enough. Now work on getting us out of here."

"We're almost out of the planet's mass shadow," Reynaldo said. "Shifting in twenty seconds."

"Good," I said, looking at the sensors. "Because we pissed off the royals." Half a dozen fighters had broken off from the fight to swarm toward us. There was no way we'd survive a concerted barrage from them.

"Shift in three, two, one," Frank announced. Reality turned to gray as the battle faded away and we shifted into shadow space.

# Chapter 11

The darkness of shadow space gave way to the real space as the *Renegade* shifted. Ahead spun Faltross Station. *Back at the beginning*, I thought. The same place I'd been captured and tortured, and then later rescued, was now our haven temporarily. A line of freighters and other smaller vessels floated, waiting for entry.

"Did we have to come here?" I asked, sitting in the cockpit.

"There are people here we can talk to and spread the word that we kidnapped the princess," Michael said. "Plus, I have some contacts here."

That piqued my interest, but I refrained from asking. The others didn't know he was a Federation officer. Did he have Federation contacts here, or were they ordinary mercenary contacts?

"Can we trust the princess to not run off?" Frank asked from the pilot's seat.

"I think we can," I said. "We came to an agreement." Indeed, in the several hours it had taken us to traverse shadow space between Zenubia and Faltross Station, the princess and I had talked...a little more. She was still standoffish toward me, but I felt confident she wouldn't bolt at the first chance she got.

"Good, because I don't want to be stuck babysitting her *and* that Gustav guy."

I groaned. How could I forget Gustav? "I'm going to go check on him," I said.

"No rush," Frank said. "It might be a while before we get in," he gestured to the line of ships waiting for entry.

I left the cockpit and made my way past where Elaina sat in the common area. She nodded to me but didn't say anything. I passed my quarters and opened the door to the makeshift prison chamber housing Gustav.

The young man, a boy, really, lay on his bunk and rolled off it as I entered. "Oh, you're back," he said. "What was all that commotion earlier?"

"They didn't tell you?" I asked. *I guess I should have checked on him sooner. He slipped my mind.* I felt a twinge of shame for talking with the princess during our three-hour shift back to Faltross Station instead of seeing to Gustav. *The princess had more reason to be upset, though. You shot down one of their royal ships.* "We ran into a little...trouble...leaving Gelcrist III."

"What sort of trouble?" he asked, a squeak in his voice.

"Nothing we couldn't handle," I hedged. Then, seeing that he wasn't buying my story, I sighed. "Okay, we had to fight off some royal ships."

"You what?" he asked, mouth forming into an O.

"I had no choice," I said. "And the princess forgave me?"

"There's a *princess* aboard?"

"Ummm...yeah. You haven't been told any of this?"

"I've been locked in here for hours."

"I'm sorry. I didn't realize it."

"It's all right. The pirates thought I was expendable too."

"I don't think you're expendable," I said, bristling. "We've just been very busy."

"It's just," he turned his gaze downward, "I can help, you know."

"I'd like to think that," I said, trying to be diplomatic. *How would my father handle this? Probably have someone spy on him.* "We can't risk letting you go until we know where the pirates are."

"I don't want to leave, though," he protested.

"You don't want to return to your mother?" I asked.

"Of course I do, but not with the Crimson Marauders breathing down my neck. I don't want to live my life constantly looking over my shoulder."

"So, you're willing to help us, to really help us, to bring down the Crimson Marauders if we return you to your family?"

"Yes."

I nodded. "That's good enough for me, but I have to talk to Michael first. He's the captain, after all."

"Where are we? I felt us shift out of shadow space."

"You can tell when a ship leaves shadow space?"

"You can't?"

"If I'm staring out the viewport, sure. Or if I'm expecting it."

"The ship starts to vibrate in a very specific way," Gustav explained. "That's the shadow drive firing up. Then there is the briefest of moments, if you blink you'll miss it, where the ship goes transparent in like a wave. That's the dephaser, it..."

I held up a hand. "I don't need to know the inner workings of a shadow drive. But I should have known you'd be a gear head. No offense." I smiled.

He smirked. "None taken."

"I'll be back. We should be docking soon. To answer your question, we're at Faltross Station. It's a crossroads, of sorts."

Gustav nodded. "It's a good place to find the Crimson Marauders. We came here after they recruited me."

*And where they captured me*, I thought. I didn't answer, just closed the door, feeling guilty locking it, and made my way to the cockpit.

"Are we getting closer?" I asked.

"Yes ma'am," Frank said. "Line's moving faster than I expected. It helps we're a small vessel. We have docking authorization."

"Good. The sooner we find out where the pirates are hiding out the better."

"I want you to come with me, Reina," Michael said from his seat behind Reynaldo.

"Okay. What about the others?"

"Frank's going to keep the engines warm, Reynaldo is going to keep the princess occupied..."

"You mean keep an eye on her and stop her from escaping," I interjected.

"Yes. And also keeping an eye on Gustav."

Reynaldo groaned.

"And Maggie's affecting repairs on the ship while we have a spare moment."

"We're going to need that sooner or later," I said.

"Let's move." Michael led the way out of the cockpit.

"Are we gearing up?" I asked.

"No. I don't want to draw too much attention. We have our sidearms, and our powers, if things get dicey."

*My gravity powers, sure. But I still don't know how to control my elemental powers.* "When we get out of here, will you teach me how to use my elemental powers?"

"I was planning on it," he said, smiling.

"Who are we meeting?" I asked.

"You'll see soon enough," he said, before exiting the bridge leading from the cockpit to the rear of the ship. Elaina sat there.

*He probably doesn't want to talk about it in front of her,* I thought.

"Heading out?" the princess asked.

"I'm going to meet my contacts and arrange for a meeting with the pirates. With any luck, we'll be directed to their base of operations."

"I know the plan," the princess said. "I still don't like being used as bait." She waved away Michael's protest. "But I understand the necessity of it. I will do what must be done to save my kingdom."

*Save it from itself,* I thought. The whole reason we were doing this was because of traitors among their guards. Who knew who among the queen's entourage could be trusted? *It's hard to know who to trust these days, no matter where you go.*

"We won't let any harm befall you," Michael said. "You have my word."

The princess snorted.

"Okay, boss, we've docked," Frank's voice came over the intercom. Lowering the ramp."

"Reynaldo will keep you company while we're gone," Michael said.

"I don't need a babysitter," she protested.

"To keep you safe," Michael insisted.

"Just hurry back. The attack on the capital could happen at any time."

Michael and I descended the ramp in silence. When we were several feet away from the *Renegade*, I leaned in toward him. "She's right you know."

"About what?" Michael asked. "The attack?"

"That she doesn't need a babysitter. She's not made of porcelain."

He stopped, turned to me, and raised an eyebrow. "Do you think I'm sexist? That all women need to be protected by strong men?"

"No, or you wouldn't have picked Reynaldo to protect her. But I feel like you're compensating for something in your past."

"You really want to get into this now?" Michael asked. "As we're walking into a hive of scum to find the queen bee?"

"Anything to avoid unpacking that clunky analogy," I joked.

He chuckled, then sobered. "I lost someone very close to me. She died in an attack and I wasn't strong enough, or fast enough, to save her."

"So, you try to save every other woman you come across?"

"I guess in some ways I do. My mother...she possesses one of the strongest personalities I've ever seen. She could make a bull bow and emperors listen. But I never saw her as needing protection. Nor my sister, for that matter. But after losing the woman I loved..." he trailed off.

*Way to dredge up painful memories, Rachel,* I scolded myself. "I understand," I said. "I lost my mother at a young age."

Michael cleared his throat. "We should be going. Remember, the capital could be attacked at any time."

I rolled my eyes but followed him further into the station. We passed through the blast doors where the creepy guy with the cigar had been standing when I first arrived there. I glanced around the docking bay but didn't see any ship that looked like the *Voltir*, the ungrateful merchant ship I'd saved. *Let's hope I don't get kidnapped again*, I thought.

*I have a solution for that,* Jarvis interrupted. *I designed a cerebral sensor array that detects foreign nerve agents and activates a nanite barrier I newly installed near the blood-brain barrier. This should detect and prevent future organic nerve agent attacks. Only a nanite-infused attack brute-forcing the barrier could...*

*Okay, okay, I get it,* I cut off my AI. *Thank you for doing that, Jarvis, but I don't need all the technical explanations. Knowing I'm safer than I was before is good enough for me.*

*Of course, ma'am,* Jarvis replied.

Faltross Station was as busy as ever, with busy corridors leading to the packed bazaar before branching off to other areas of the massive commercial station.

Michael seemed to know where he was going, for he led us without hesitation toward Green Sector. From my limited knowledge of the layout of the station, Green Sector was the warehouse district. We stopped in front of a door proclaiming the business within to be "Galdut Industries."

"This is a known shell corporation the Crimson Marauders use," Michael explained. "Let me do the talking."

"Fine by me," I said. I would be more prone to bash heads first and ask questions later. *Time for finesse this time,* I thought.

Michael activated the door and led me inside.

A gruff-looking woman with dirty blond hair sat behind what looked like a makeshift reception desk. "What do you want?" she asked without preamble.

Michael cleared his throat. "We have some cargo your associates will want to know about."

"Not interested," the woman said without hesitation.

"Really? Because it is a *very* precious cargo."

"Like the crown jewels valuable," I chimed in.

Michael shot me a sharp glance.

The woman's eyed us, eyes narrow. "Well, spit it out. I don't have all day."

*It looks like you do, though*, I thought, looking around the office she occupied.

"We've heard your associates are looking for the crown princess of Zenubia. We have her."

The woman's eyes went wide before she could compose herself. "How do I know you have her?"

"Would we come here telling you we did if we didn't have her?" Michael asked.

The woman sniffed. "You'd be surprised. Wait here." Without waiting for acknowledgment, the woman left her desk and hurried down a corridor to a room near the end.

"What are the odds this is a trap?" I asked, ready to draw my pistol and upon my power in an instant.

Michael shrugged. "It'll work."

"That's not an answer," I said.

Michael's reply was cut short by the door the woman had entered through sliding open and a tall, burly man walking toward them. The woman followed at a distance, as if afraid of him.

"You have the princess?" he asked without preamble in a deep, booming voice? "How do I know?"

"We can offer video proof," Michael assured him.

"Then do it," the man demanded.

"One moment," Michael said, holding up a finger. He reached into his pocket and removed his communicator. "Reynaldo, are you there?"

"Yeah boss, what's up?"

"Our associates would like to see the princess. Can you turn on the video function and show her to us?"

"Ummm..."

*Don't blow it for us,* I thought. If Reynaldo decided to talk back, or play the white knight and refuse, our cover, and our only lead to the pirate base, would be blown.

"Sure, boss. One second. She was...being rowdy so I had to knock her around a little."

He must have muted the line, because I expected to hear very vocal protests from the princess. Instead, an uncomfortable number of seconds later, he came back on the line. "Ready when you are."

"Switching to video," Michael said. He held up the screen so I and the hulking pirate could see.

I held in a gasp, barely.

The princess had her hands bound and someone had stuffed what looked like a dirty grease rag into her mouth.

*Maggie must have lent him that. She is* not *going to be happy about being asked to do this.* I harbored no doubts that she was truly bound, only playing a part, but still, the indignity of it seemed to manifest in her eyes with the defiant glare she shot toward the camera.

The pirate leaned in, studying the bound and gagged prisoner. He reached into his pocket and consulted his datapad. "It's her," he concluded. Then his face contorted into the most hideous thing I'd seen in a while...a smile. "Well done, friends."

"Thank you," Michael said, shutting off his communicator and stuffing it into a pocket. "We want to deliver her in person. You understand. The prestige of it."

The bigger man nodded. "Of course, of course. Judith! Get these mercs the coordinates for the staging base."

The secretary jumped, frightened by the man's shout. "Of, of course," she said, hurriedly typing something into her computer. Moments later a paper was printed out. "Here are the coordinates."

"Make sure you tell them Big Rico sent you," he said, holding out a hand. "It's been a pleasure."

Michael smiled, though I could tell it was forced, and shook the man's hand. "The pleasure is ours. I'm ready to stick it to the Zenubian kingdom once and for all."

"Yeah," I chimed in. "Death to all royals."

Big Rico raised an eyebrow at that, then let out a belly laugh. "A woman after my own heart. I'd get the drinks and toast to that if we weren't in a hurry. Best be on your way."

Michael inclined his head. "Let's go." He led me out of the room. He waited to speak until the door had slid closed and we were halfway down the hall. "Nice touch, there at the end."

"You don't think it was a little excessive?" I asked.

"Nah. I think it reinforced our ruthless intent. Let's head back and then take off."

*I wonder what awaits us at our destination*, I thought.

# Chapter 12

"Seek the door again and draw upon your power," Michael instructed me.

Standing there, eyes closed, I once again sought the "door" in my mind behind which sat the elemental power I'd recently acquired. It was second nature to reach for my gravity powers, but the elemental powers, those were harder to access. After several seconds of hunting for it, I found and opened it. Elemental power flooded me, seeking release.

"Good. Form a flame above your right palm. Hold it steady."

I channeled the power like before, this time down a single arm, and envisioned the flame forming. Heat washed over my hand.

"Open your eyes," Michael said. "You'll need to learn how to use your magic with your eyes open. You can't exactly fight with your eyes closed. Well, you can, but it's much more difficult."

"I feel like I can sense everything," I said, keeping my eyes closed. "I can sense you, and your power, like a pillar of energy, and I can sense the engines and the others, they have an energy, only lesser."

"Every living being has an energy inside them," Michael said. "Whether we detect the electrical energy of their nerves or something more primal or supernatural, I don't know. My...some of the greatest researchers of history have been unable to definitively answer that question. Regardless, not every threat will be visible via such elemental senses. You may use them, but do not make the mistake of relying solely on them."

"Of course," I said. "Just like I would rely on my eyes and ears, I can rely on more than one sense."

Michael nodded. "Indeed. Now open your eyes."

I obeyed, eyes flickering from the flame floating above my palm to Michael's blue eyes. "What now?"

"Now you must learn to control it. Conjuring the elements is only half the battle. Really, only a quarter of the battle. The true challenge mages face is not summoning their magic but controlling what they summon."

"I can imagine," I said. "My gravity powers were similar. I could summon the power, but it took time to control it effectively."

Michael nodded. "Indeed. This challenge of molding the elements to our wills is often why mages specialize in one or two elements. Trying to control all of them equally well makes for a mediocre mage because it's like," he paused in thought for a moment, "trying to juggle five balls instead of three. That's a poor analogy, but you'll soon see what I mean."

"You're going to have me try to control more than one element?"

"Of course," Michael said, a smile softening his words. "Perhaps not today, but at some point, you will have to at least try. It's important to learn your limits during practice so that you don't push yourself too hard in battle and pass out."

I frowned. "But if it's a matter of life or death wouldn't I *want* to push myself to the breaking point?"

Michael smirked. "It's better to live to fight another day than sacrifice yourself needlessly. But you're right, if it were a matter between say, the fate of the human race and your life, and pushing yourself to the point of destroying yourself was the only way to save the human race, then perhaps there would be a case for such an action. But that is hypothetical, and I'm not here to teach philosophy...I don't have the patience for it."

I chuckled at that. I could see philosophy being boring to the man. "So, what is the next step, *master*?"

He raised an eyebrow. "I'm hardly a master. But I'll allow it. Compress the flame into a small point."

"How?"

"How do you compress gravity singularities?"

"I just...envision them shrinking."

"Then try the same with the flame. Collapse it in on itself or condense it into a smaller space."

I closed my eyes, preparing to do that.

"No," Michael snapped. "Eyes open."

I groaned but complied. I turned my gaze upon the flame that floated above my palm. *It's about the size of a basketball. I should try to condense it into a baseball.* I envisioned it shrinking, resisting the urge to close my eyes.

At first, nothing happened. But then, the ball of flame started shrinking. Slow at first, it became more noticeable the more I stared, and the longer I concentrated, until what had been a basketball-sized ball of flame was now exactly the size I had envisioned. I smiled and looked at Michael.

He nodded. "Good, if a little slow. In combat, you won't have time to concentrate for long. Such maneuvers must come as second nature."

"It is only my first day," I said, feeling somewhat deflated. The flame extinguished. "Second if you count the day I woke up from my wounds."

"I know," Michael said. "But we're heading toward God only knows what at the pirate base and it would be of great use to the team if you had control of your powers before then."

"I'll try harder, then," I promised.

"Summon the flame again and this time you're going to try 'casting' it away from you. Think of it like throwing a baseball."

"Okay." I summoned the flame again with my mind, noting that this time it seemed much faster. "How do I cast it?"

"Much like you did when you shrank the flame, you're going to envision propelling the flame away from you."

"Oh, like I do with my gravity powers," I said. "Let me try." Remembering to keep my eyes open, I "pushed" the flame and it moved...right into the wall. It crashed against the wall and the bindings of magic keeping it together shattered. Heat washed back toward me. "Oops."

Michael smirked. "A good first try. You *want* it to move fast in combat, but next time try moving it slowly toward your target."

"Yes, sir," I said, offering a mock salute.

"This is a good opportunity to teach you about the opposite of heat - cold."

"Going back to elementary physics, are we?" I asked.

"Very funny. I'll allow you to close your eyes this time. Focus on the patch of wall where your fireball hit. What do you see with your senses?"

Taking advantage of permission to close my eyes, I reached out and studied the wall. Waves of reddish-orange energy cascaded away from the wall, gradually fading the further the waves wen. *That's consistent with physics*, I thought. Heat tended to radiate until the object reached the temperature of objects around it. "The heat is radiating away from the wall. As expected."

"Yes, but that's not important. This next part is. You are now going to accelerate the radiation of the heat. You're going to suck out as much heat from that location as you can as quickly as you can. Even the ambient heat."

"Which would freeze that spot," I said, opening my eyes.

"Correct. It's easier to do this with an object, such as a wall, than with air alone. You can summon ice bolts, technically, but it requires a combination of drawing in water droplets and freezing them at the same time. Far too complex for you to manage today."

*Like one of those mages did to me back at the Holy See*, I thought. *Okay, draw the heat from the wall.* I closed my eyes again and found a warm spot. Even in just a few seconds, the waves had decreased in intensity. I studied the situation, wondering just how I would suck the heat away from the wall faster. Behind the waves of heat, I found a lattice of energy, like what I had summoned to form into flames. I tugged on that lattice and pulled it toward me. The heat waves continued radiating, but they were detached from the wall now! I folded the lattice in on itself to form a circle and the heat stayed inside for a moment, before radiating out the top and bottom.

"Good. Now ignore the heat for a moment and look at the wall," Michael ordered. "This time with your eyes.

I turned my gaze to the wall and gasped. Frost covered it, and it looked brittle, as though it could shatter at any moment. I closed my eyes, unbidden, and studied the spot. There was an absence of heat, of energy, though waves of heat from the air around that spot seemed to be slowly filling it up.

"Such a magical maneuver could be used to shatter a piece of a hull of a ship if you had enough energy to freeze the entire structure and then applied enough force to shatter it. Interior walls would be easier to break."

"Why aren't such maneuvers used more often in space warfare?" I asked.

"It's dangerous, for one. A mage would need to get right up to the hull, and that would require energy shields on the enemy ship to be disabled or turned off if you were planning an ambush. There are far easier ways to breach the hull than potentially sacrificing limited supply mages."

"I see. And that probably applies to most use of magic in war, doesn't it?"

Michael smirked. "Yes. Even before the Federation took to the stars, mages were used sparingly. The grandiose efforts take grandiose amounts of energy, and mages are not limitless in power. They were often held in reserve to counter enemy mages. Neither side in a conflict wanted to be caught with their mages too weakened to defend against a large counterstrike, as the loss of lives could be catastrophic."

"I thought the Empire didn't use mages," I said.

"Oh, they *use* them," Michael said, emphasizing the word "use." "Literally. The Federation employs mages, in a partnership. The Empire enslaves mages. They view them as inferior to non-magical humans and use them as a Marine might use their rifle - as a weapon, a tool to kill people."

"That must be why I hadn't heard that before," I said. "It's probably a dirty secret."

"Yes, it is. The Empire propaganda pretends it doesn't happen and the Federation doesn't like to shine a light on the matter, lest radical groups in the Federation get ideas."

"Funny how the Federation likes to hide things too," I said. *Right, Dad?*

"I don't know of any government that doesn't hide something from its citizens," Michael said. "Knowledge is power, but it can also be dangerous."

"It should be up to the citizens to decide that, though," I said. "Too much coddling can create a society of complacent citizens that allow their nation to crumble around them."

"It is a balancing act," Michael agreed. "No easy answers in governance."

"What's next?" I asked. "For my training." *I'm not going to get further into a civic argument with the man.*

"I think that's enough training for now. Eat up, get some rest, and get ready. We don't know what is waiting for us at our destination. We could be in for a fight."

"I'll be ready," I said.

# Chapter 13

The gray of shadow space gave way to the black of space as the *Renegade* shifted out of shadow space. Empty space.

"There's nothing here," I said.

"We should be waiting for a signal," Michael said, brows furrowed. "It's possible this is a relay point."

"You mean we go from here to another point?" I asked.

"Yes. It's a safety mechanism to ensure we aren't followed."

"I'm monitoring all the channels for any communication," Reynaldo said.

"And I'm ready to turn around and get the Hell out of here," Frank said.

"Don't be such a baby," Reynaldo said. "It'll be fine...probably."

I cracked a smile at that. Humor in the face of a dangerous situation was a coping mechanism for many people.

The comm crackled to life. "Unidentified vessel, state your business," a male voice demanded.

"This is the *Renegade*," Frank said, showing no hesitation at using our actual ship name. He had made a point of arguing that we should use a fake transponder and name, but Michael said this would be more authentic. "Transmitting ship ID. We have the package our mutual friend told you about."

"Stand by," the voice said. The comm muted for several seconds. "Transmitting shift coordinates now. Shift to these coordinates, then await the transmission of additional instructions."

"Understood," Frank replied. "*Renegade* out." He closed the comm and let out a sigh.

"Once we arrive and ensure it's not another relay point, I'll transmit the coordinates to my allies."

"Allies?" Frank asked. "What allies?"

"The Federation," Michael said.

"How do you have allies in the Federation?" Frank asked, sounding suspicious.

"It's a long story," Michael said, voice even. "I'll explain later. Right now, we need to get to these coordinates and find the pirate base."

"Coordinates are input," Reynaldo said. "Relatively close location."

"Initiating shift," Frank said, sounding like he was speaking through gritted teeth. "Let's hope there's not more duplicity waiting for us at our destination." He initiated the shift and our surroundings shifted from black to gray.

I stood up. "I'm going to check on the princess."

"It won't be long before we arrive," Michael cautioned.

"I know. I won't be long."

I left the cockpit and made my way back to the common area of the ship. There I found the princess sitting across from Gustav.

"Enjoying your freedom?" I asked Gustav.

He smiled. "Yes. Thank you for putting in a good word with the captain."

I nodded. "At this point, even if he doesn't fully trust you, he trusts there's no way for you to sabotage our efforts now."

"I wish I trusted your captain's plan as much as you do," Princess Elaina said.

"I won't let anyone hurt you," I assured her.

"And what if you're incapacitated?"

"It would take a lot to incapacitate me," I said.

"I will do my duty to protect my kingdom, but I don't have to like it," she replied.

"We all make sacrifices, sometimes," I said. "Sometimes the greater good outweighs the individual good." *Ugh, that sounds like something my father would say*, I thought.

"We're about to shift back to real space," Frank's voice came over the ship-wide comm.

"I'm sorry, I have to go," I said before racing back to the cockpit and retaking my seat.

Shadow space gave way to real space and from my seat in the cockpit, I looked out at a sea of asteroids. "An asteroid belt?" I asked.

Michael nodded. "It's a common hiding place for pirates. Shields them from unexpected shifts near their base, giving them extra warning, as well as physically hiding the base from prying eyes."

"So, do we just fly in or what?" I asked.

The comm crackled to life. "*Renegade,* I am transmitting a path through the asteroid field. Follow the path exactly to avoid damage to your ship."

"Understood," Frank said. "*Renegade* out." He closed the channel.

"Look at that. Considerate pirates," Reynaldo said. "They don't want us to damage our ship."

"More likely, they don't want to damage our precious cargo," Michael said. "Before we go in, Reynaldo can you open a long-range communication?"

"Sure, one second..." he trailed off. "Uh, boss, there's a problem."

"What kind of problem?" Michael asked.

"We're being jammed."

"Jammed?" Michael repeated. "How?"

"It's a signal coming from the asteroid field. It's preventing the use of the shadow array."

"Shit," Michael said. "We can't call for help, then."

"Not unless they're within range of our local transponder. And I'm assuming they're not."

"Correct. And the pirates would pick up on even encrypted local channels and get suspicious even if they were."

"So, what's the new plan?" I asked.

"Can you pinpoint the exact source of the jamming?" Michael asked Reynaldo.

"It looks like it's being relayed from multiple locations to create a broad wave of jamming effect. I'm working to triangulate the primary source."

"What are you thinking?" I asked.

"Should I get moving?" Frank asked.

"Yes, get moving," Michael said. "We don't want to make them suspicious." He turned to me. "Once we identify the primary source, I want you to float out and destroy it while we continue on our path. Do you think you could do it unnoticed?"

I nodded without hesitation. "Yes, you can count on me."

He smiled. "Good. Reynaldo, put the primary signal generator on the map and compare it to the path we've been provided. When we're at our closest point, Reina will eject and make her way toward it."

"Got it, Boss," Reynaldo replied.

"As soon as I disable that, they're going to know something is up," I said. "That could put you in the line of fire."

"Let us worry about that. The second the interference drops I'll signal the Federation. You get back to us and then we'll get the Hell out of here while we wait."

"That's our plan?" Frank asked. "Evade until help arrives?"

"Essentially," Michael said.

"Great plan," Frank said, deadpan. "Now the princess might die for real."

"We needed the princess in order to be invited here," Michael pointed out. "We won't let anything happen to her."

"That might be out of our hands," Frank said as the *Renegade* reached the edge of the asteroid field. "Let's wait and see what is awaiting us."

The *Renegade* swerved and dodged as Frank expertly navigated the ship through the asteroid field, following the invisible twisting, curving line the pirates had transmitted.

"Is this really the most direct route?" I asked as he banked sharply to avoid a giant oncoming asteroid.

"No such thing as a 'direct route' in an asteroid field," Frank replied. "How are your 'friends' going to get in here, anyway?" he asked.

"The plan was for them to shift out where we were, then make their way in," Michael said. "Now...they'll do the best they can to shift out at our location."

"That could get messy," Frank said.

We sat in pensive silence for several minutes as Frank continued his careful navigation.

As we cleared a particularly large asteroid, I gasped. "Is that a moon?"

"It's not a space station," Michael said.

Indeed, it was an actual moon of rock, by all appearances. The asteroid field wrapped around the moon, being kept in a steady orbit that left a clear space around the moon for hundreds of kilometers. Dozens of pirate capital ships floated in that space. Hundreds of fighters flitted in packs as well.

"Looks like there's a base on the moon," Reynaldo said, zooming in with the external camera and overlaying it on his side of the cockpit.

"That's a heavily fortified base," I said. "And those fighters...looks like they're gearing up for a fight."

"That moon base is right where we're headed," Frank chimed in.

"Why would their fighters be deployed?" Michael asked.

"Think they're on to us?" Reynaldo asked.

"No. That doesn't make sense. If they knew who we were, they would have attacked at any point along the way."

"Maybe they're getting ready to depart?" I asked.

"I don't mean to interrupt our speculating," Reynaldo said, "but there's the signal generator," he pointed to a floating station hundreds of kilometers away from the surface of the moon. "We're nearing the closest point."

Michael looked at me. "You ready?"

"I was reborn ready," I said, smirking at my wit. I rose from my seat.

"You gonna gear up?" Reynaldo asked.

"There's no time, is there?" I asked.

"We're thirty seconds away," Frank said. "I can't slow too much, or they'll get suspicious."

I smiled. "I'll be fine." I made my way out of the cockpit and to the airlock. I stepped into it, sealed the inner door, and activated the outer door. With a whoosh, the air evacuated, and I allowed myself to be carried with it into space. Within a second the *Renegade* was past me and on its way toward the moon base.

I floated in the silence of the void and waited for several seconds. *I hope they don't notice me.* None of the packs of fighters prowling the space deviated from their course. Satisfied I hadn't been detected, I bound myself to a gravity ball I sent traveling at medium speed toward the signal generator, a speck compared to the moon in the background. Even at medium speed, I soared through space, the lack of air preventing my hair from whipping behind me.

No pirate vessels floated near the signal generator. *I'm in range*, I said mentally, Jarvis translating my words into a signal being transmitted short-range to the *Renegade* via a military-grade encrypted channel.

"Any time now," Michael said. "We're waiting for you."

I drew upon my power, preparing to send a singularity soaring toward the signal generator. It would collapse and the signal would vanish.

*I am detecting multiple distortions nearby,* Jarvis warned, interrupting my summoning.

I frowned. *What sort of distortions?*

The answer to my question came a moment later as space visually "twisted" in various locations, a hallmark of shadow drives tearing holes in space-time to allow ships to exit shadow space. *Could it be the Federation?* I wondered. Had they somehow tracked the *Renegade* even with the jamming?

My answer came a few moments later as the ships coalesced into reality. They were not Federation designs. *Those are Zenubian ships,* I thought, shocked.

"Attention pirates," I powerful transmission reverberated through my brain, courtesy of the open channel between me and the *Renegade*, "this is the HMS *Eminence*. We have learned that you have the crown princess in your possession. You will return her at once or face the full fury of Her Majesties Navy."

*It seems like it might* be *their whole navy,* I thought. Dozens of capital ships had emerged, likely equaling or outnumbering the pirate vessels. *And certainly outclassing their ships.*

"How did they follow us?" Frank asked over our channel.

"It's impossible," Maggie chimed in. "I scanned the ship, and with that jamming in place, no signal would have gotten out even if we had been bugged."

"That leaves only one possible explanation," Michael said.

*The pirates leaked the location, once they knew the princess was on her way,* I said through the link, my mind spinning and putting together the pieces.

"It's a trap," Michael said, finishing my logic. "They deliberately released the princess's location and waited for us and the royal navy to show up. The question is, why?"

"Could they want to attack the home world?" Frank asked. "Zenubar would be exposed."

*But why would they want us to bring the princess here*, I asked. *And why leave military ships behind?*

"I think their trap is more elaborate than we've thought," Michael said. "Reina, focus. I need you to disable that signal generator, *now*." The urgency in his voice startled me.

Not asking for clarification, I summoned a gravity orb and sent it floating toward the signal generator blocking the *Renegade's* shadow array. Moments later it contacted the hull of the floating generator and space distorted as my singularity crumpled the relatively small structure. It was far smaller than capital ships I'd destroyed. *It's down*! I shouted. *But what are you worried about?*

"Sending the signal," Michael said. "I'm worried the pirates have something more sinister planned."

*Additional distortions detected,* Jarvis chimed in, speaking to me.

*Shit. We've got company,* I warned over the link. *Could the Federation be here this soon?*

"That's not the Federation," Michael predicted, voice grim.

Indeed, the distortions representing shift-points twisted to coalesce into new ships. Pirate ships.

# Chapter 14

S*hit*, I thought to myself. *Michael was right to worry.* Dozens of new pirate ships, some bearing the markings of the Crimson Marauders, other bearing the markings of unknown to me pirate organizations, appeared behind the Zenubian fleet. *They're surrounded,* I said over the link.

"I was worried about this," Michael acknowledged. "They can eliminate the Zenubian fleet in one swift blow, giving them a clear shot at Zenubar."

"And we played right into their hands," Reynaldo chimed in.

A wave of gravity erupted from the moon, more than the moon itself could generate. *They've activated something,* I said. *It increased the mass shadow of the moon.*

"Gravity well generator," Michael guessed. "Experimental, and I don't know how the pirates got their hands on one, but it's used to stop ships from shifting in or out of specific areas of space."

*They're well and truly trapped now,* I said.

"They're fucked, you mean," Frank said. "And us too. I say we high tail it out of here."

"No," a new voice said, sounding like it came from the cockpit but near the back. "Those are my people out there. I won't abandon them."

"Princess, please go back to..." Michael began.

"So, you plan on leaving them to their fate?" she asked.

"Of course not," Michael said. "But we need to survive until reinforcements arrive."

*But the Federation fleet can't shift in with that gravity well in place,* I noted. *I can see the gravity waves with my power. It extends to the inner edge of the asteroid field.*

"Is there something you can do to counteract the gravity effect?" Michael asked.

*No,* I said. *But I can destroy the generator.*

"There are three fleets between you and the moon," Frank pointed out.

*Do you have a better idea?* I asked, trying to inject as much sarcasm as possible into my reply.

"I won't ask you to do this," Michael said. "It's going to be dangerous."

*You don't have to ask me,* I said. *It's a sacrifice I'm willing to make.*

"You're a noble warrior," Michael said.

*Don't tell anyone,* I said. *Especially my father,* I thought to myself. I summoned a gravity ball and cast it toward the rear of the newcomer pirate fleet. *Where are you guys?* I asked.

"We're between the inner pirate fleet and the moon," Michael said. "And I think the jig is up. We've got a squad of fighters headed our way, and they're hailing us. We're going to have to stop the link for now."

*Be safe,* I said, instructing Jarvis to sever the link. *All alone now.* Something I was used to.

I increased the speed of the gravity ball dragging me along and aimed it toward the first of the ships in the group of newcomer pirate ships. *No mercy.*

The gravity ball slammed into the hull of the first pirate ship, a corvette-type ship with a snake symbol painted on its hull, and the hull crumpled around the ball, twisting and being sucked into the mobile singularity. I followed closely behind it, remaining untouched by the debris left behind. I avoided looking to the sides or too closely at what was sucked up. Yes, the pirates deserved what happened to them, but I didn't have to watch their bodies be ripped apart by the singularity or jettisoned into space.

I passed through the wreckage of the first destroyed ship and reoriented myself toward the source of the gravity waves emanating from the gravity well generator on the moon. *Keep your eye on the prize.* I didn't want to get distracted by reveling in destruction. The royal fleet would still be in peril if reinforcements didn't show up.

I reoriented my gravity ball toward the source and sped up once more. I smashed through a second pirate ship, a frigate by my estimation, and found the royal navy ahead of me. *Gotta avoid destroying any of their ships.* I dodged a harried battle cruiser, then a hail of laser fire from a pair of fighters flashed past me. *Shit, they're on my tail.*

I didn't want to hurt any more royal navy fighters this time around, so I increased my speed further. A normal human would have been crushed by G-forces of acceleration long ago, but I was no ordinary human. I glanced over my shoulder as I flew, seeing the gap between me and the royal fighters increasing. Moments later they broke away and went after a pair of pirate fighters instead.

I skirted around several more royal navy ships before I reached the inner circle of the Crimson Marauder fleet. Dozens of fighters tangled in dogfights, while missiles streaked across the void. Nothing else blatantly targeted me and I continued at my new top speed through a single enemy corvette, eyes still on the prize.

Breaking through the Crimson Marauder fleet I found the moon ahead of me. I stopped and scanned the void, looking for the *Renegade*, but couldn't identify them immediately. *I can't worry about them.* They said they were being pursued, so they could have gone in any direction.

The source of the gravity well surge lay ahead of me. As I neared, lasers flashed through the void around me as I moved forward, with the gravity ball absorbing direct blows from in front.

*Should I blow through the moon until I get to that point?* I wondered. No, destroying the moon could cause a lot of damage to ships in the area, including friendly ships. I decided to land on the moon and try to find it to surgically destroy it.

I sailed toward the moon and swept over the surface, then released my hold on the gravity ball and bound myself down until my boots were on the surface of the moon. I looked around and found a complex to my right. I lifted into the air and bound myself in that direction, floating several feet above the surface of the moon.

The complex reminded me of a series of towers, with a central tower leading to a large satellite-dish-type-structure. Waves of gravity cascaded out from the satellite dish. *There's my target*, I thought. I accelerated toward it, staying low to the ground.

The earth erupted beneath me, knocking me into the air and off course. I lost my concentration and the gravity ball evaporated. *What the hell was that?* I thought. Then I saw it. Multi-colored streams of magic flowed from two towers flanking the satellite dish emitter. The streams coalesced again, and this time lightning flashed toward me as quickly as light. It flashed through my body before I could muster a defense and caused my muscles to lock up. It lasted for several seconds before letting up.

I dropped to the moon's surface and bound myself downward to keep from floating up. I closed my eyes and focused on the "door" in my mind behind which my magic resided. I opened the door and felt magic flood me. *Now what magic to use to hit back at them,* I thought.

Summoning heat, I stretched my arms out and tried to create a fireball. I saw the streams of magic like red ropes coalescing into a ball of heat, but no reddish-orange flame formed. *Idiot, you forgot oxygen.* Without oxygen to ignite, there would be no flame. I released the streams of magic forming heat. It would be too difficult to maintain with no air to ignite.

I could counter with lightning, as they did, but they could block that. *Do they know that I have magic?* I wondered. The last time their mages had battled me, I had killed them all and absorbed their magic, leaving no witnesses.

*What if I pull the magic into me as I did before?* I wondered. I prepared a gravity well in front of me and walked forward, bracing for lightning to be sent toward me again.

It came moments later and instead of hitting me this time it flashed into my gravity well. But this time instead of allowing the energy to be drained into the void, I rerouted the raw power into my body. Flows of energy streamed up my arms and into my body. My hands glowed with power. Then I released the gravity well and summoned light between my hands. Not light born of fire, but raw photons of energy, stripped from the lightning and drained from the gravity well into my body.

I spread my arms wide, fingers splayed, palms toward the enemy towers while splitting the pool of energy so that a glowing light hovered inches from my open palms. Then I *pushed* the energy down my arms, feeling as though I was draining my life force in some ways, and twin beams of white light a meter or two in diameter lanced out faster than my eyes could track and collided with the towers. Within moments, the metal began melting under my onslaught. I spread the beam and it washed over the top of each tower. Though space absorbed all sound, I felt spurts of energy, minuscule compared to the power I'd unleashed, signifying what I assumed was the power of those two enemy mages extinguishing.

*Well, that's over*, I thought. I looked up toward space. The battle raged on, with the embattled royal navy looking to be worse for wear. *Don't worry, I'm coming*, I thought. I floated above the surface of the moon once more and streaked unchallenged toward the satellite dish representing the gravity well emitter. Several moments later, I landed atop the emitter. Gravity waves buffeted me, keeping me steady but not crushing me due to my power. *Now how to destroy this thing.* I tried to summon a gravity ball, but the waves disrupted it. *So, I can't use my power to destroy it.* I studied the metal of the emitter. *What about magic?* I thought.

I closed my eyes, knelt, and touched the cold metal. In my mind's eye, I delved into the metal and "saw" the molecules of the metal, barely moving. *So, to melt the metal, I would need to agitate the molecules. How do I do that?* I needed the energy to feed such an endeavor, as the emitter was a several meter high structure of pure metal. I couldn't draw upon my reserves, as I didn't think I had that much magic in me, and Michael had warned me of mages burning themselves out by drawing upon too much magic at once.

*Wait. The gravity waves are a form of energy? What if I did the reverse of what I did with the lightning?* Could I convert the gravity waves into energy used to manipulate the molecules of the metal? *It's worth a shot,* I thought. Worst case scenario I would go to the base of the emitter and try to topple the device and hope it destroyed it.

Closing my eyes, I let the waves of gravity wash over me, then started sucking them in. I became a human black hole, essentially, and drew in the gravity waves. The waves hammered me and absorbed into my body, filling me with gravitic energy. I felt it swirling within my mind, threatening to overwhelm me. I envisioned it like a thread, one which I sent through the door in my mind representing my elemental magic. Then I drew upon that same elemental door and felt the same energy returning but now instead of gravitic energy it was elemental.

*There we go,* I thought. I channeled the elemental energy down my arms and back into the body of the emitter. It flooded the emitter, leaving my body. I reached out with my mind again and delved deep into the metal. I seized upon the molecules and infused them with energy. Slowly the molecules started shaking. I pushed more energy into the emitter, drawing upon the gravity waves continuing to emit from the device and converting them into elemental energy I then continued surging into the structure.

At first, nothing happened, but then I felt the emitter shaking. The shaking continued until the structure shook violently. I leaped free as the emitter shut off abruptly as the electrical connection feeding it power shut off, heedless of where I floated. I kept my mind focused on the structure and infusing it with every last bit of energy I could. Several seconds later I felt drained and drew my mind back.

A hulking pile of metal slag sat in the space where the emitter once stood, barely recognizable.

*Jarvis, open a channel to the* Renegade.

*I am trying, ma'am, but I cannot find them,* he replied.

*Does that mean...* I trailed off, not wanting to put it into "words."

*They likely turned off their transponder to avoid becoming a target for as long as possible. It is possible to send an encrypted broadcast a short way using the internal antenna within my hardware suite, but I estimate it will not cover the entirety of the space between this moon and the inner edge of the asteroid field.*

*Okay, do it anyway.*

*Transmit at your leisure.*

*Attention* Renegade, I began, *the emitter is down, if you hadn't noticed. Good to go.*

No reply came.

*I don't want to just sit here like a sitting duck.* I bound myself upward, no longer inhibited by interference from being so close to the gravity well emitter, and soared toward the battle lines, hoping to help.

"Renegade to Reina," Michael said through the link. "It's good to hear your voice."

I smiled and would have let out a shout if I hadn't been floating in the soundless void of space. *Now we wait for reinforcements?* I asked.

"That's the good news and why I couldn't respond right away," Michael said. "They should be here any moment."

*Multiple distortions detected,* Jarvis alerted.

*Here comes the cavalry,* I thought.

# Chapter 15

T hee distortions representing shift-points twisted to coalesce into new ships. Federation ships, this time.

Ships ranging from cruisers to corvettes and everything in between appeared in clusters above and around the battlefield. I estimated two dozen capital ships had arrived between the two pirate fleets, bolstering the military might of the royal navy.

Several of the capital ships disgorged swarms of fighters while launching immediate barrages of missiles, lasers, and bullets into the void toward the pirate fleets.

My heart skipped a beat as I saw the largest of the ships appear. *The* Nightblade *I thought. My father's ship.* Of course, there was no guarantee he was on his flagship, but still, I wanted to stay away from it. *I want to stay away from all of them.*

*Where are you?* I asked the *Renegade.* I would be safe from scrutiny aboard my ship. *No more theatrics today*, I thought. If I went bursting through pirate ships now someone within the Federation would notice and possibly piece it together with the supreme commander's daughter's powers. The time to rejoin my team had come.

"How about we come to you," Michael said. "Focusing on your location. We'll be there shortly."

"Hang in there, princess," Frank said.

I smiled. *Take your time. I'm just relaxing.*

I watched the battle ensuing while I waited. Husks of several capital ships, including the two I had destroyed, floated through the void, but they were husks from ships of all three factions, as the Federation had right away lost a corvette to a ramming effort by a pirate frigate.

A speck in the distance resolved into the *Renegade* a few minutes later. They slowed their descent and I bound myself toward the hull and walked toward the airlock. After the outer door had closed and the room pressurized, I re-entered the ship and made my way straight to the cockpit.

The princess, Elaina, sat in my seat but rose as I entered. She hugged me. "Oh, you're cold," she said.

"It's cold in space," I said, stating the obvious but smiling to soften the words.

"We're glad to have you back," Michael said, smiling.

"I'm glad you didn't die," Frank said.

"It was boring without you here," Reynaldo said. "Just Frank being broody and Michael being quiet."

"So, I'm boring now?" the princess asked.

Reynaldo flushed. "No! Of course not!" He performed a seated bow. "Your beauty rendered me speechless."

Elaina snorted, then turned back to me. "Your seat."

"Where's Gustav?" I asked.

"Manning the guns," Michael said.

"Nice. I see you've grown to trust him."

"We're all in the thick of it together, now."

"Can I please get back to my ship now?" Elaina interrupted.

"As soon as the fighting dies down, Your Highness," Michael said.

"Then what are we waiting for?" she said. "Let's help win this battle." She departed the cockpit without waiting for a reply."

Michael sighed. "The end of this battle can't come soon enough. Frank, take us into the thick of it."

"I'm on it," Frank said, directing the *Renegade* back toward the fighting.

"What's the *Nightblade* doing here?" I asked.

"Oh, that's not the *Nightblade*," Michael said. "That's its sister ship, the *Shadowblade*."

"How original," I said. *Did my aunt name these bloody ships? At least it's not the* Nightblade. Less chance of someone recognizing me or my powers.

The *Renegade* surged back into the battle, with Gustav manning the batteries and Frank juking this way and that to fire the forward batteries or launch missiles.

I was more than happy to watch the battle instead of actively flying around in the void. Not only was it safer, but it was also far less exhausting.

A few more Federation ships had taken serious damage or been destroyed, mixed with several royal navy vessels in the same status, but the pirates were taking a beating.

I felt a surge of gravity coming not from the moon but the direction of the Federation fleet. "Is that another gravity well projector?" I asked.

"Yes. The *Shadowblade,* as well as the *Nightblade*, are both equipped with gravity well projectors to prevent hostile fleets from escaping into shadow space."

"I didn't know that," I said. I'd spent weeks aboard the *Nightblade* and never even heard whispers of such technology. *I guess my father didn't trust me.*

"It comes in handy when you want to eliminate a pirate cluster once and for all. It's why I requested a ship with such capabilities."

Twenty minutes later, the battle was over. Smaller pirate ships had fled into the asteroid field, pursued by Federation or royal navy fighters, while the larger ships were destroyed or surrendered.

The comm crackled to life. "Starship *Renegade*, this is the captain of the HMS *Eminence*. I understand you have some precious cargo for me?"

Michael smiled. "Priceless cargo, captain. We'll head to your ship and dock immediately."

"Excellent." The comm channel closed.

A SHORT WHILE LATER, the *Renegade* touched down aboard the HMS *Eminence*. The ramp lowered and Michael and I accompanied Elaina off the ship.

A royal entourage met us at the base of the ramp, with a grizzled, gray-haired captain meeting us. He bowed low to the princess. "Your Highness, it is good to see you safe."

"Thank you, Captain Fineas," Elaina said, inclining her head. "These brave mercenaries risked their lives to keep me safe. I would see them given any resources they require as thanks."

My eyes widened. *Money? I could use some money.* I opened my mouth to speak...

"That won't be necessary," Michael put in before I could utter a word. "A firm friendship between our two nations is thanks enough. I am not a diplomat, but I hope that the actions of the Federation in the royal navies great hour of need will factor into Zenubia's decision to join the Federation."

The princess smiled. "I am quite certain it shall."

"What of the traitors in your midst?" I asked.

The captain cleared his throat. "After the attack on her highness, military intelligence reviewed the battle and discovered secret communique regarding the attack. They used it to track down and apprehend all of the traitors."

"Excellent," the princess said. She turned to me and smiled. "We may not see eye to eye on everything, but it was nice knowing you, Reina. If I can ever be of assistance to you personally, please let me know."

I considered asking for reward money but thought that would be a bit tacky now that Michael had declined. He *was* the captain after all. Instead, I smiled graciously and offered a slight bow. "It was my pleasure, Elaina. Likewise, if you ever need any help, just ask."

Elaina held her smile and shifted her gaze to Michael. "And you, the mysterious captain who is not a mercenary. Thank you again for your help. It is clear the Federation took great risks to keep my kingdom from falling into anarchy."

Michael smiled but said nothing, merely inclining his head. After a long moment, he spoke. "We should be going. The *Shadowblade* is expecting us."

# Chapter 16

"I'm leaving you in command," Michael said less than an hour after we'd docked at the *Shadowblade*. Behind us, transports and fighters took off and landed as the cleanup from the battle continued. The *Renegade* sat off to one side.

"Me?" I asked, raising an eyebrow.

"What? You don't think you're up to commanding the *Renegade*? Care for me to promote Reynaldo or Frank instead?"

"Aye, give me a command, Sir," Reynaldo said. "I'd enjoy having her swab the decks."

I pointed a finger at him. "Just for that, I'll take the command."

Michael smirked. "I never doubted it."

"You think you know me so well?" This time I crossed my arms. Sure, we'd had an adventure together, and he's trained me in magic, a little, but that didn't mean he knew me.

"I think I'm a decent judge of character."

"While you go jaunting off into space? Where are you going, anyway?"

He shrugged and offered a wry smile. "It's classified."

I laughed. "Of course it is. The military never changes." That revelation still surprised me. An officer, leading a ragtag band of mercs on a secret mission. I half expected Isabelle to come shifting out of the shadows any moment. *You know if you tell him who you are, he'll tell your father.*

"You could come with me. Enlist. Again."

I snorted. "Yeah, right. The military isn't for me anymore, and probably never will be in the future."

"Hence why I know the *Renegade* will be in good hands."

"How do you figure that?"

"Because you won't abandon her or give her over to the Federation." He nodded toward the other three members of my crew, four if you counted Gustav, who stood off to one side talking in low voices. "They deserve that."

"And will we meet again? You and me?"

He averted his gaze, focusing on the military transport waiting on the landing pad. "I don't know. My CO isn't happy about how things shook out and well...they're going to try to put me on a short leash going forward."

"You, on a short leash? Why don't you just stay out here with us?"

"And leave the Federation?"

I shrugged. "Why not? The galaxy is a big place, Michael. Come with us and see the galaxy."

"If I were anyone else, I would," he said cryptically. "But I have duties, Reina. Duties to my homeland and my family that, as much as I want to, I can't abandon that duty. There's a threat coming, I don't know when or where, but it's coming. I swore an oath to be there when the threat emerges, and I can't abandon that either."

I felt an urge to ask what threat, but fought it down. It was probably just a ploy to get me to re-join the Federation military. Pique my curiosity and get me to tag along. It reminded me of the Krai'kesh bullshit my father peddled. "Well, while you're jumping at shadows, I'm going to make a difference," I said. I held out a hand. "It's been an honor."

He smirked and clasped my hand. "The pleasure has been mine." Then, to my surprise, he leaned in and kissed me on the lips. It was a quick kiss, finished before I had a chance to react, then he gave me a mock salute and made his way toward the Federation transport ship.

*May we one day meet again*, I thought. The man who had taught me magic and saved my life a time or two. A man I had grown to care about.

A whistle behind me jerked me out of my reverie. "That looked like a good kiss," Maggie said as she stepped up beside me. "If I may say so, Sir."

"Don't call me that," I said. "I'm not an officer."

"You're the captain of our ship, now," Frank said from my other side. "Makes you the boss, Ma'am."

I cringed. "Can you just call me 'Reina'? Or 'boss'? Or maybe 'captain?'" *I'll have to tell them my real name eventually*, I thought.

"Oh captain my captain," Reynaldo began, walking past Frank toward Michael's ship before turning to face us. He offered a flourishing bow. "We shall follow you to the ends of the galaxy."

"Stalkers," I said, softening the words with a smile. My gaze flickered once more to the Federation transport as a figure I thought was Michael walked up the ramp. The guards at the base of it saluted him. *Back where he belongs,* I thought.

"Where to now, Boss?" Maggie said.

"To find work. We're low on credits. Being heroes of Zenubia doesn't pay well, evidently." I shook my head and turned my back on the transport, and Michael. "Reynaldo, find us a safe harbor away from this ship - we've stayed here too long already. Maggie, check our supplies and make a list of essentials. Gustav, go with her. Frank..." I rattled off a list of orders as we made our way back to the *Renegade*, berthed on the far side of the docking bay. *Life goes on.*

# Don't miss out!

Visit the website below and you can sign up to receive emails whenever Dayne Edmondson publishes a new book. There's no charge and no obligation.

https://books2read.com/r/B-A-ZEND-PTFY

BOOKS 2 READ

Connecting independent readers to independent writers.

Did you love *Space Commando*? Then you should read *Emergence*[1] by Dayne Edmondson!

[2]

**Aliens have invaded the Milky Way.**

Captain Martin and his fleet at the opposite end of our galaxy is all that stands between the emerging ancient aliens and certain **destruction of humanity**. Even with the help of powerful magic, the alien menace may be too much to overcome.

Elsewhere, Agent Hague chases down rumors of a secret cult after an assassination attempt on the president of the Federation's life.

With the emergence of the long-foretold aliens, the Federation stands on the brink of destruction. Can Captain Martin and his allies hold the line? Can Agent Hague uncover a plot within the Federation?

---

1. https://books2read.com/u/brgddE

2. https://books2read.com/u/brgddE

A tribute to Star Wars books of old, and the first book in a new trilogy in the existing Seven Stars Universe, "Emergence" is set nearly two thousand years after "Shadows Fall" and features cameos from many of the longer-lived heroes of ages past.

Click now and jump into the adventure today.

Read more at https://www.darkstarpublishing.com.

# Also by Dayne Edmondson

### The Dark Tide Trilogy
Emergence
Eclipse
Ruin

### The Mageborn Saga
Mageborn
The Cursed Tower
Halls of Light

### The Magical Madelyn Mayfield
Madelyn and the Unicorn Beach

### The Seven Stars Universe
Ghost Ranger
Space Commando

**The Shadow Trilogy**
Blood and Shadows
Time of Shadows
Shadows Fall


**Standalone**
The Complete Dark Tide Trilogy
The Complete Shadow Trilogy


Watch for more at https://www.darkstarpublishing.com.

# About the Author

Dayne Edmondson lives in southeastern Michigan with his wife and two young children, a boy and a girl. He writes part time and works a day job.

His books can be read in this order:

**The Shadow Trilogy**:
1. Blood and Shadows
2. Time of Shadows
3. Shadows Fall

**Mageborn Saga:**
1. Mageborn
2. The Cursed Tower
3. Halls of Light (coming 2019)

**The Seven Stars Universe**:
1. Ghost Ranger (coming 2019)

**The Dark Tide Trilogy:**
1. Emergence
2. Eclipse
3. Ruin

Dayne enjoys reading, writing, the occasional video game, watching TV with his wife, walking and spending time with his children indoors or out.

He writes and reads science fiction and fantasy. Some of his favorite authors/books include Robert Jordan, Brandon Sanderson, (almost) all the Star Wars EU books, Elizabeth Haydon, Christopher Nuttall and more.

Read more at https://www.darkstarpublishing.com.

## About the Publisher

Dark Star Publishing is a small-press publisher of science fiction and fantasy novels. They place particular emphasis on books written **in** the Seven Stars Universe (the universe created by author and owner Dayne Edmondson).

For more information, visit https://www.darkstarpublishing.com

www.ingramcontent.com/pod-product-compliance
Lightning Source LLC
Chambersburg PA
CBHW031127210626
46816CB00015B/1151